The Hidden Chamber

A Legendary Love Story

Virgil Ballard

Order this book online at www.trafford.com
or email orders@trafford.com

Most Trafford titles are also available at major online book retailers.

© Copyright 2013 Virgil Ballard.

All rights reserved. No part of this publication may be reproduced, stored in a retrieval system, or transmitted, in any form or by any means, electronic, mechanical, photocopying, recording, or otherwise, without the written prior permission of the author.

Printed in the United States of America.

ISBN: 978-1-4669-7679-5 (sc)
ISBN: 978-1-4669-7678-8 (e)

Trafford rev. 02/25/2013

Trafford
PUBLISHING®   www.trafford.com

North America & international
toll-free: 1 888 232 4444 (USA & Canada)
phone: 250 383 6864 ♦ fax: 812 355 4082

The Hidden Chamber

A Legendary Love Story

Virgil Ballard

Order this book online at www.trafford.com
or email orders@trafford.com

Most Trafford titles are also available at major online book retailers.

© Copyright 2013 Virgil Ballard.
All rights reserved. No part of this publication may be reproduced, stored in a retrieval system, or transmitted, in any form or by any means, electronic, mechanical, photocopying, recording, or otherwise, without the written prior permission of the author.

Printed in the United States of America.

ISBN: 978-1-4669-7679-5 (sc)
ISBN: 978-1-4669-7678-8 (e)

Trafford rev. 02/25/2013

www.trafford.com

North America & international
toll-free: 1 888 232 4444 (USA & Canada)
phone: 250 383 6864 ♦ fax: 812 355 4082

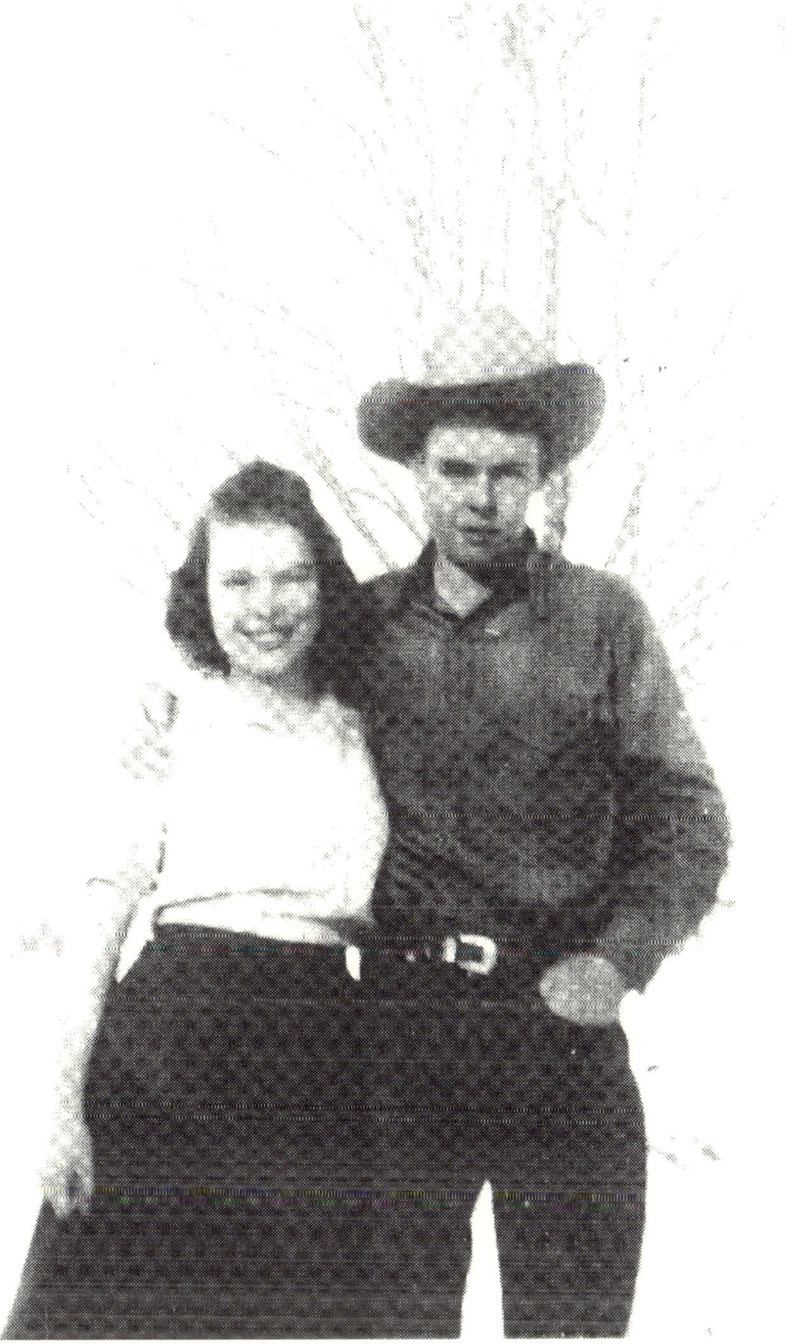

The Hidden Chamber

The year is 2098. The place is the western United States. A renowned archivist has stumbled on a remarkable story of love spanning the last half of the Twentieth Century and the beginning of the Twenty-first. His search for the truth leads him through an intimate tale of hearts lost and a never ending quest for love.

Far more than a mere romance, this book, based on a true story, reveals the incredible resilience of the human spirit to love through great barriers of time and space. This is a magnetic, enticing story that has both young and mature readers clamoring for more.

THE HIDDEN CHAMBER

It all began in 1942
Ruth & Virgil had their sights
set on the future together . . .
But Ruth's Grandmother Estella
had other plans. Therefore the
future had been changed for ever!

This Book Is Dedicated To:
The Families and Descendants
of
Ruth and George Saunders
&
The Families and Descendants
of
Virgil & Caryl Ballard

By Ben Rivera

There's probably no thing that angers me more than ignorance. I feel so strongly about this that it makes my hands tremble whenever I hear people use that tired, worn-out saying: "There's no such thing as a stupid question."

Well, believe me, the next time I hear someone say that, I'm going to do everything I can to avoid getting upset. You see, there are lots of stupid questions being asked all around the world this very minute-hundreds of lame brained questions-so many of them, in fact, that sometimes I wish I didn't have to answer my phone, or even to check my emails.

People always ask me stupid questions because it's my job to hear them, and I spend far too many hours each day answering such queries. I feel so strongly about this that I announced my opinion on this matter, although many people already had been well aware of my philosophies in this regard. Anyway, that's when I issued a state press release on my office letterhead, featuring the official

Great Seal of the State of Nevada. The press release proclaimed my official opinion that "most questions are stupid."

Needless to say, since I'm a high-ranking public official in state government, there was an immediate public outcry-amid heated and vocal public demands that the governor of our state fire my worthless butt.

A few talk-radio hosts even latched onto the issue. Dozens of angry callers phoned in to these stations, collectively yelling-and agreeing, in a sense-that I should be tarred and feathered. The most frequent comments were essentially that "Ben Rivera is a jerk, and a fool. He's a perfect example of why government fails, a mindless bureaucrat." The phone lines sizzled and the airwaves burned up as discussion intensified, especially on Marcus Brushie's "Firing Pin" program on KKOH-AM Talk Radio in Reno, and on the "Let's Nail 'Em" program hosted by Jim Collagian on KLAS-AM Radio in Las Vegas. To my credit, though, I refused to get caught into the trap of these ratings-minded broadcasters, who invited me onto their programs to give my version of what happened. Off-air, through my office spokeswoman, I had refused their invitation, essentially telling those proverbial "radio-Gods" to go to hell. I knew that if I went onto those programs, the snot-nosed, wicked-tongued broadcasters would chew me up, like a wolf caught in a steel trap.

This time, I was the one that outsmarted them. It's important here to note that on another occasion, three years ago, I once had fallen victim to their evil-minded ways. So, this time, for the life of me I wasn't about to allow such a vicious ambush to happen again. And who could blame me? Sure enough, there are those of you who remember that three years ago, I fell into a trap that these same radio stations had laid out. That time, the issue was an official state article I had written, dispelling a myth that the dome on Nevada's Capitol Building, built in 1878, was once embossed with a thin plate of silver. Since childhood, most folks who grew up in Nevada, nicknamed the Silver State, were taught to believe that the Capitol, designed by Marius T. Woodmen, and built by the Plumas-Humboldt Construction Company, had its original dome caked with a super-expensive, thin plate of silver, which had been mined from the heart of the Comstock in nearby Virginia City. Our state's school children, during mandatory Nevada History Classes in the seventh grade, had been taught since the mid-1930s that daring vandals cut the silver-plated dome out of the Capitol Building in the middle of the night of Nov. 2, 1894; two days after the proud state celebrated its 30th anniversary of statehood.

One would have thought an atomic bomb had blown, when my article was published three years ago, attempting to dispel or eradicate what I hailed as that "Great Dome Theft Myth." As far as I was concerned, any sound-minded person should have agreed with me, since I proved thorough detailed research-and actual historical building-permit records-that the original dome was comprised of nothing but tin. In 1905, this myth had been born, and became "reality," due to an article written by curmudgeonly columnist Franklin Miller in the Reno Gazette-Journal, which at the time served the biggest city in the state. It seems, from what I could determine in researching that column and various other articles penned by Miller, that he had a tendency to stretch the truth beyond the limits of believability. Nonetheless, a gullible public accepted Miller's reporting as "fact", and his stories soon became mandatory in some history textbooks.

Anyway, a few days after my article on the dome fiasco appeared, I was foolish enough to go onto those talk-radio stations for a simultaneous broadcast in Reno and Las Vegas. Ignorant of the press at the time, I got lambasted, burned worse than a pig roasted with an apple stuck in its mouth. Irate callers had the nerve to complain that I was ignorant-perhaps the biggest fool in state history-for being naive enough to write such an article. The issue became so vocal, in fact, that the following day the governor summoned me into his office to discuss the matter. By the time I left my office to go to his, word had reached my staff that the governor was either going to fire me-or even publicly sanction me, or perhaps worst of all, demote me to a staff-level position. To my good fortune, though, right before I arrived at his secretary's desk, the governor had been summoned from Carson City to Las Vegas for an emergency meeting of the State Economic Development Commission, on a vastly different issue having nothing to do with the state dome. Afterward, perhaps because it's the nature of politics, the issue of my writing that Dome Scandal article somehow seemed to have been forgotten-and the situation never was brought up again by his administration.

And since then, to their credit, despite rumblings from a handful of politicians-particularly Nevada state assemblymen Dick Rowley and Morgan Cartwright from the Las Vegas area-each one of the 17 school districts statewide have stopped teaching the once-heralded Dome Legend as being factual. Under order of various school administrators, a directive accepted by the governor, any mention of the legend in school textbooks was either edited out altogether or mentioned only briefly, along with a bold footnote that the "former myth has since been disproved.' Such changes indicate that no matter how much the general public claims to hate me, I'm generally respected by most of my peers in state and local governments, at least by those who matter most.

Yet all this fails to take away the fact that this latest controversy, and eventually my statement about the public being "stupid" all stemmed from a mere poem. That's right. Just one tiny poem written long ago, "Looking Back," led my staff and me to launch an intensive 3-year-long research project. And indirectly, at least the process of our researching the poem's history, eventually led to my write the "stupid people," press release, followed of course by the international controversy that won't seem to go away.

If you're one of the few people who haven't heard of or about the poem by now, then at least feel satisfied that in this publication you'll be among the first to get the story straight-laid out in the following pages for everyone to discover. Nonetheless, although it's a poem written some time ago, and even though I've never met the author, this poem has caused me nothing but grief and heartache-and, interestingly enough, rubbed out my efforts to achieve personal happiness as well, at least for a time anyway. Even so, whether I like it or not, that single poem, and several others by the same author, is now recited in romantic cafes around the world, from Russia to Paris, and from New York City to Honolulu.

As far as I can determine, other than folks who saw a popular motion picture about the poem, most people never even heard of them, until I had the audacity to make a public issue of their true origin. While all this might sound compelling and mysterious, the important thing here-at least from my perspective-is to know that those poems led either directly or indirectly to my professional downfall, or at least the fact I'm about to lose my job.

Now, here, in this pamphlet, sort of a romantic novella intermixed with a mystery, I have to admit I'm not necessarily an eloquent guy. As far as I'm concerned, I'm perhaps one of the world's worst speakers, both in person and in public. That remains my conclusion, despite the fact I earned a doctorate in history from the University of Nevada a quarter century ago, and even though some people consider me one of the most eloquent people they've ever met. To be sure, my communication skills are more precise, persuasive, and downright good when it comes to putting my thoughts, findings and convictions on paper in the written word. However, when it comes to vocalizing my thoughts, I'm about as eloquent as a newborn chicken with a tissue stuffed into its beak. At least this is the way I think of myself, while others insist quite the opposite is true-that I'm perhaps even more eloquent than Abraham Lincoln. It's no stretch of the imagination to say many people have compared me to him in numerous ways, which you'll soon discover.

Be that as it may, like I say, my press release on "ignorant questions" issued two weeks before I wrote the initial draft of the document or miniature biography you're reading now, still failed to convince a majority of the public that most queries are predictable. All along, I'm sure you might find this pamphlet downright compelling. In places a smattering of laughable scenes erupt. Despite such points of humor, whether intended or not, this official proclamation originally issued by my office is intended to be considered as super-serious in both nature and content.

With this in mind, parents are cautioned, advised under no uncertain terms to keep this booklet away from children-particularly youngsters under the age of 18. Although nothing within the confines of these pages is to be considered X-rated in nature, those who discover the true meaning of these poems-and of why they were written-are likely to get heart palpitations. I doubt if even lovesick teenagers could even understand. As far as I can determine, some readers became enraptured with this true-life tail, for there can be no denying that this story-well documented in every respect-is chock-full of passion and human desires, of both the loving nature and of the physical nature, although not necessarily resolved in every regard.

If you're human, if you're the curious sort, you might be wondering how such passion, how such love-at least those attributes emitted by the true author of these poems-could have resulted in my "downfall" from my lofty state position. Since it would be impossible to accurately and concisely give all these answers in a few sentences, suffice it to say here that anyone who wants the "truth" about those poems must read further.

With this clearly understood, now, is the ideal time issue several basic warnings: First off, put this book down now, if you think "romance" is nothing but nonsense. And drop this book, and throw it in the trash right away, when you get to detailed sections about love, missed desires, and late-night dreams, if you think they're corny. But, truly, they aren't. And somehow, at least judging by testimonies of those many people who have already cruised these pages, herein rests a story that must be told. Without question, not giving these details fully and honestly would be an outright crime.

"Thank the Lord, you've had the courage to tell this story," one reader told me, calling my office immediately after this pamphlet was first published-before this second update that you're reading now. "Mister Rivera, I had no idea what those poems meant to the world, until you had the courage to tell the truth about how, when, and why they were written. I had never even heard about the author, sir, until your booklet came out. Mister Rivera, once I started reading it, I couldn't put it down. And I find myself reading it again and again, and I've been buying copies for all my relatives and friends, and most of them-just about all of them-feel exactly the same way as I do. This is an amazing story."

Needless to say, of course, I've felt vindicated by such reactions. And yet, until a certain point at least-as you'll discover soon enough, I also somehow felt sad, as if I never quite could achieve my own happiness. How would my life had turned out, had I not been stupid enough to investigate the heritage of those poems in the first place? Would I have remained in my current "prestigious" job for many years to come, rather than preparing to leave my office in just a few months as I am now, on the day I write this?

Be that as it may, at least from my perspective, anyway, it's a story you should tell your children when they're old enough, and they-in turn-should tell their children, and their children's children. Yes, without exaggeration, this is that kind of story, an eternal tale that should be remembered throughout the entire universe, for all time. Now, I'm not just saying this here in my own defense, in some sort of effort to save face for myself-since, at least in part, the primary purpose of this booklet was from its conception-and it remains today-to document my reasons for issuing the "people are stupid" press release.

Now that I've managed to get these basics out of the way, at the start, here, I must admit that my press release on the "stupid questions" issue was intended to be quite the opposite from comical. I issued that press release because I seriously want people to "think," because I'm tired of ignorance in our world, and I want people to know that even more important than being "smart," we'd all be better off if everyday folks would concentrate on matters of love, rather than hate, deceit and ugly, unadulterated greed. Looking back, though, I must confess that the "offensive" press release in question made no mention of love, but instead proclaimed this notice: "People are no longer allowed to ask stupid questions of state government officials. Most of the calls our state government office receives are from stupid people, and we'd like to officially ask such callers to stop bothering us once and for all. In this office, we have much more important work to do, than to chat with idiots"

You'd think that people would have understood the underlying message of what I was trying to say. But I had no such luck. Our office phones started ringing-literally-off the hook, the morning after the press release was issued. One would think this would have been a typical press release, the kind of boring, everyday notices that reporters immediately chuck into their garbage cans. But, no, this time, I couldn't be so lucky. This time, newspapers, TV stations and radio stations around the world reported the press release, word-for-word. Yes, the media is a mighty, fire-breathing dragon with enough energy and might to burn out a mere government office with a single breath. Before putting out that statement, I had been ignorant enough to miscalculate both the strength and scope of the news industry.

As you may have heard by now, sparked by the resulting publicity, it seems that stupid people from all over the world felt motivated to call my office the very next day. Callers asked perhaps the most stupid question of all-why we, or more specifically why, I, Ben Rivera, had the audacity to issue such a statement. Well, 43 minutes after the office opened that morning, our Ear-Phone lines shut down, due to what the fine folks at SBC Nevada Bell explained as "system overload." Sadly, though, at least from the perspective of my office staff, and of myself, this malfunction didn't prevent lots of stupid people from marching into my office that morning to demand answers. Headstrong and steadfast in my convictions, I had my department's official state spokesman, Ann Breen, Public Information Officer of the Nevada State Archives

Office, answer any questions from reporters and other leaky-nosed creatures of that bent.

This reaction on the public's part only served to convince me even further that what I had done in issuing that press release was the "correct" thing to do. Yes, people are ignorant, they're pea-brained, and through the years they've asked more idiotic, insignificant questions of me-and of my overworked office staff-than I'll ever care to remember. More than ever, I'm convinced that people are always struggling for happiness-average folks everywhere-and they never achieve what they want-because they fail to stop and smell the roses, or to recognize love when its staring them between the eyes.

* * * *

"Why on earth could you feel that way, Ben?" you might ask me, echoing dozens of similar statements I've heard from an irate public in recent days-ever since I've made my opinions known on this matter. "Ben, how can an educated guy like you, an expert at gathering highly detailed historical information, actually announce to the world that you believe 'most questions are stupid?' For heaven's sakes, have you gone crazy, Ben? Are you losing your mind"?"

Well, if the truth was told, I'm as sane as any fellow could ever be, and the more this heated public argument intensifies-the more strongly I feel about the matter. Goodness knows I'm not going to dignify those complaints, by giving just one, simple answer at this point. You see, my official title is State Archivist of the State of Nevada. Now, that's a pretty fancy-sounding job, I suppose, isn't it? At least that's what most people seem to think when they first hear the phrase.

But just what is that, anyway, a state archivist? Don't worry if you're not able to give an accurate answer at this point, because if you're unable to say what a state archivist is, or what a state archivist does, you're not alone. Most people haven't got the foggiest notion of what or who an archivist is, and they never give it much thought anyway-primarily because they've never heard of the job. Nonetheless, it's a fancy enough title to get me plenty of attention, at least when people first hear about the position. Indeed, that mere phrase "state archivist" always seems to get me instant credibility-or at least that was how everyday folk reacted before this current heated controversy began. But I'm getting a bit ahead of myself now. I promise to give you all the in-depth details a little further on in this pamphlet. First, though, I think it's important for me to "set the scene," so to speak, so that you can understand where I'm coming from on this issue, and how all this public debate erupted in the first place.

At the start, please keep in mind that each state has only one "official state archivist." A state archivist is the person who keeps the official historical records of a state. The job of a state archivist is to hunt down the "truth,' or at least to get details as accurate as possible, in chronicling the history of a community, state or country. Needless to say, that's a mighty important responsibility, especially as people worldwide become increasingly interested in history.

And topping all that off, giving me even more prestige, so to speak-while being ever-so-humble on my part-I suppose this is as good a place as any for me to also let you know that I'm also President of the American Association of State Archivists. To put all this in perspective, keep in mind that besides having my official state title, I'm head of this non-profit organization of state archivists from all 50 states.

Our association, commonly known among archivists as the AASA (pronounced "ass-ah"), meets twice yearly for education purposes. Members often exchange vital information on how to perform our jobs, and even more important-we frequently work together, or cooperate in research, when documenting historical events that transpired from one state to another.

I must say from deep within my heart that I'm proud of this association and its many important accomplishments. On a vote of 43 to 2, with three abstentions and two absent, I was elected to a third consecutive two-year presidential term last April at our bi-annual meeting at the Hilton in Denver. Maybe it might impress you that it was a near-unanimous vote. But I admit, I don't give a hoot if you care or not.

What might impress you is that I got a standing ovation at the conclusion of my so-called inaugural address. Even the two members who hate my guts with a passion found themselves clapping and cheering for me, as I sat down after my speech. Just as important from my perspective, the moment that banquet ended lots of association members came to the dais, where one-by-one many of them told me that it was a historical speech that will be quoted and re-quoted again and again for centuries to come.

I'm not exaggerating one bit here when I say this. But I'm getting ahead of myself again. I'll recap the speech, toward the end of this document. Then, you can judge yourself. For now, rather than skipping through to that point, though, it's essential for you to get all necessary details, point-by-point, especially those facts about of my intensive research into the background and emotions of Mister Ballard, the guy who wrote those poems that happen to be getting so much worldwide attention these days.

Similarly, rather than try to spill out all details about Mister Ballard on this one page, let me lay out the facts, piece-by-piece in the pages that follow-in the same chronology that my staff and me discovered details. It's essential for me to dole out specific, integral details this way, carefully, methodically and accurately, as completely as possible. Along the way, please accept my humble assurances that each detail has been carefully researched and documented. Many of the facts were checked and then rechecked, in some cases numerous times, by myself and by various others. In some instances, this seemed necessary, because some details appeared almost too unbelievable to be true. Yet, like I say, everything has been documented, certified as accurate.

Nonetheless, despite what you might already have detected is my obvious excitement, particularly as it relates to this project, I'm going ahead with my plans to retire from my state job next July 17, and I'm already counting the days till I'm able to walk out the door for good. Now that it's official, since everyone who needs to know has been informed that I've submitted my retirement papers, I'm making this big confession.

I hate my job. That's right, I hate it with a passion. I can let it all out, what I think of this position. At this point no one can get me fired anyway. You see, it was the process of researching Mister Ballard's history that I gradually, over time, came to realize this fact-to the point that I yearned to leave my job with all my heart. This is not to say or to imply anything "bad" about Mister Ballard or about the "love of his life." To the contrary, I have nothing but respect and admiration for the man. This is so true, in fact, that if I were to get one chance to meet any single person in all of history, it would be to spend a single day with Mister Ballard and with his "true love" as well.

Well, that's a pretty tall statement for me to make, now, isn't it? When asked such a question, I suppose most people would answer that they'd enjoy spending the time with Jesus, Buddha, or Mohammed. But instead of choosing those spiritual icons, no matter how much I love them and respect them, I'd choose to spend my special time with the late Mister Ballard. "Why?" you might ask me, especially when considering the fact he was an "unknown"-at least in matters of the world scene-when he died many years ago. For now, the only direct answer I have to those who would ask such a question of me is to urge them to read this document in its entirety, and only then, I hope, will my reasons for retiring become obvious.

* * * *

Well, herein rests an ideal opportunity to take a deep breath and to relax, for you're about to get all the details. At the start, feel free to think of me as a fool or as an idiot for quitting my job. I don't care what you think of me, but I do care-sincerely-about what you might think of Mister Ballard and of his true love. I must admit, now, that when I first heard of Mister Ballard I thought little of him, and gradually over time, I confess, I started to hate him. This was not a mere hate, mind you, one of those situations where one person says "I hate your guts and want you dead." No, in this case, really and truly, I honestly hated the guy with all my heart, although I've never met him and never will in this lifetime. Initially, at least, I hated Mister Ballard, for the grief he had caused me, for all the heartache, and all the intense research I was forced to conduct just to discover the "truth" about him, and for what working on this research project did to my own home life. It has been said, by some, that I "lost myself in this research project that

I changed forever. And I'll have to admit that's the case. I'm bitter, mad, and angry, even since the initial publication of this booklet got many of the facts laid out for everyone.

Yeah, despite the many positives that have come forth as a result of this project, by some people at least, I'm perceived as a "whiner," especially among folks who haven't read this document. I know what you might think at this point, probably something like, "laugh, and the whole world laughs with you, Mister Ben Rivera. Cry, and you cry alone." As if that statement were a predictor of things to come for me, my upcoming retirement was announced just seven weeks before I issued the "stupid people" press release. Since then, there have been those who've insisted I'm a crybaby, and a wimp. Just three months ago, shortly before the initial publication of this booklet, and right before my re-election as president of the archivists' association, editorials in two of Nevada's most prestigious newspapers, the Reno Gazette-Journal, and Las Vegas Review Journal, blasted me for giving my opinions on "stupid people" as I prepare to leave my state job.

"Already the butt of jokes both nationwide and around the world, Ben Rivera is a prime example of everything that's wrong with government," the Gazette-Journal said. "Not only is Rivera an embarrassment to state government, and to the state of Nevada as well, he has brought unneeded and unnecessary national and international ridicule upon the Silver State. At a time when Nevada struggles with the vital and necessary work of diversifying its economy, the last thing we need is for some bureaucratic loud-mouth like Rivera to make our beloved state a brunt of jokes everywhere."

The funny thing is, and this is the God's-honest truth, such criticisms fail to sway me in the least. If anything, I've become more resolved than ever to get my point across. Sadly, though, there's no sense in me granting interviews on this matter, since reporters invariably get it all wrong 100 percent of the time anyway. By submitting to interviews with print journalists, and even with the electronic media for that matter, I would simply bury myself even deeper in this unwanted crevasse of misunderstanding.

Even so, still determined to defend myself, and to set the record straight, so to speak, I decided to write this small booklet. Lots of people got upset when the initial printing of this document was published at state expense. I was able to authorize these printings, because I have the authority to designate how such monies are spent within my division, at least when it comes to so-called "discretionary funds" for anything I deem "necessary emergency research, required to ensure the accuracy of historical accounts of Nevada history."

Well, as you might expect, complaints intensified once word of this publication got around, yet only from those who never bothered to read it. Please keep in mind that this is the "second printing" so to speak, with some minor revisions from the first. Updates were necessary, especially on the page you're reading now, to get the word out that this publication has emerged as an unexpected, and overwhelming international success.

At this point, I must confess that I'm proud to say that due to burgeoning, and unexpected demand for this publication, we've had to cease actual printed versions and start distributing these revelations on the Internet in e-book formats. I remain convinced that after learning the facts as they're laid out here, people will be able to make up their own minds on the matter. Every single detail you'll see on the pages that follow has been well documented, checked and rechecked for accuracy. My 15-person staff did much of the work.

CHAPTER ONE

The first thing people notice about me when they meet me is my height, at exactly 6-foot-6-inches to be precise. The other thing about me is my beard, which at first glance makes people think of Abraham Lincoln, who was two inches shorter than me. These reactions usually last for only a moment or so, until people realize that unlike that famous president I'm chubby and lack any sort of quick wit that helped him gain fame. Making matters worse, at least for me, I seem to lack common sense and can only wish I had a seasoned, wise mind such as his. Yes, good old Abraham gained a well-deserved reputation as a seasoned statesman, while I'm thought of-at least by some-as a sort of kook or a crackpot, since my work entails mystery and intrigue, delving into details of the past.

Like I say, I obtained my doctorate in history a quarter century ago, in 2073 to be precise, at the University of Nevada, Reno. I was born in 2048 in San Francisco. An only child, I revolted against my doting parents, and upon my graduation with lackluster grades from Fremont High School on Powell Street downtown, I finagled my way into an out-of-state scholarship, a program designed to help put worthy but needy teens. I mention all this because people might want to know where I'm coming from, basics of my background, in order to understand my intense motivation in seeking out details of Mister Ballard's personal history, and of his motivations. Suffice it to say that I've always been a rebel of sorts, especially due to the fact my father continually spoke of his own dreams-of how we were going to be rich someday, but we never were; of how he was going to get himself a decent job one day, but he never did; and even that he intended to attend some of my high school sports events, but he never did. It always seemed my family was always on the verge of achieving our dreams, but somehow those aspirations never came true.

While the story you're about to read mentions me quite a bit, ultimately it's about Mister Ballard and the love of his life. In setting the scene, at least as it relates to me, I want you to know that I disliked my parents, and if the truth be told, I don't much care for people as a whole for that matter. Isn't that odd, when you consider people often refer to me as the most kind, loving and caring person they've ever met. Don't ask me why, because I can't say for sure-but I give constantly to what I deem worthy charities, such as programs that feed starving children. What a paradoxical situation. Here I am, a guy whose very lifeblood entails delving into every aspect of other people's lives from many decades ago-as if I cherish them, as if I adore everything about them so much that I'll go to any legal ends necessary to discover the truth about them-and yet I treat people who work for me as if they're scum. Then, for the life of me, I really can't say why, I donate to many worthy charities and even volunteer in programs such as being a non-paid orderly at Southern Nevada Memorial Hospital.

"Ben, I have to tell you that you're just about the biggest ass I've ever known," my secretary, Beverly, told me just last week-just as I was headed out of the office, to mail another $5,000 check to the Feed the Children Campaign, formerly known as C.A.R.E. "And believe me, Ben, I've known plenty of people, so that's saying a lot."

My instant reaction was to fire Beverly on the spot for insubordination. Yet hand-tied in such matters, I'm privy to the fact she and everyone else on my staff is a civil service employee. Once they pass their probationary periods, their jobs are protected by stringent regulations under the State Human Resources Code. In some respects, Beverly reminds me of my girlfriend from way back in high school, Patty Carnahan. Like Beverly, Patty had long red hair, a body that would have made Marilyn Monroe jealous, and a heart of gold, although feisty and headstrong. The interesting thing is, Patty and I never got together, we never dated much, and we stopped seeing each other for good about one year before graduation. Passionate and madly in love with each other before our separation, we had spoken frequently of how someday we would marry, and of how we would make our livings, and how important we were to each other. But one summer she went on vacation with her family in Hawaii. During that period, our Cyber-Mails back and forth to each blasted across InfoSpace like lightning. But suddenly, Patty's Cyber-Mails to me stopped, about a week before the fall semester was to begin for our senior year. Sensing her Digital-Units had crashed, at first I thought little of this lack of response. But, then, I began blasting her mails daily, telling of my anger and frustration. None of my queries to her were returned, because-like I say, and I'll say it again-all questions are stupid anyway.

I spent the first week of my senior year in high school moping around our house, actually an apartment unit above the Wal-Mart-Sears Department Store off Market Street in the heart of downtown San Francisco. After Patty disappeared from my life, I'd spend mornings crying alone in my bed, refusing to go to school after my parents left for their jobs at the Marina Emporium. My room turned into a mess, littered with papers and food wrappers-a signal to everyone that I definitely was in a terrible funk, since usually I'm known as being more meticulously clean than Felix Unger from "The Odd Couple."

That incident, I suppose, my breakup with Patty marked the beginnings of the person who I am today. You'll understand why much later on in this report. You probably started reading this, I'm sure, expecting me to write all about my research into the history of Mister Ballard. Yet, to know about my research, you first must develop a keen understanding that my life has been a repetitive pattern of yearning to achieve, yearning to find happiness, an aching sensation that I need to achieve personal and professional goals-none of which quite seem to be accomplished. I say all this here because it's an integral part of the story. To this end, despite all my yearnings to find happiness, and although I strived to learn to "truly like" others, for most of my life I never seemed to reach those objectives.

For instance, while I detested most of these people, the folks I work with, there are those who've earned lots of my professional respect in recent years, especially for their arduous efforts in researching Mister Ballard. Like me, all of them had heard little or nothing about him until our research project began. Like I say, our 3-year-long research project on him entailed intense research, which usually lasted more than 10 hours daily. Throughout it all,

I kept thinking how easy all this would have been, if one of my predecessors-Mister Guy Rocha, Nevada State Archivist in the late 1900s and early this century-had done all this research himself, during that latter part of Mister Ballard's life.

If that had been the case, Rocha could have talked to many people who knew Mister Ballard first-hand. But, of course, sadly at least for me and for my staff, during Rocha's era this poet, except for his superior work as a real estate industry executive, had been a relative unknown at least in the local, national and international scheme of things. I'm sure Guy Rocha would have nailed every detail down, even better than I have. On other research projects, it was Rocha who dispelled such myths as who invented the Ferris wheel in Nevada, the comings and goings of Mark Twain when he wrote for the Territorial Enterprise in Virginia City from 1868 to 1872, and even whether President John Fitzgerald Kennedy made a secret rendezvous with actress Marilyn Monroe at the former Mapes Hotel in Reno while she was in town to film the "Misfits" co-starring Clark Gable in 1960.

I mention Rocha here since it was he who laid the important groundwork in starting my office, and putting in place its basic traditions that continue to this day. Unlike Rocha, who worked alone in a single office at the Nevada State Library Association Building just east of the Nevada State Capitol Building in Carson City, my office has a 15-person staff, off the Boulder City Highway in Las Vegas, 480 miles from Rocha's former stomping ground. The fact the state library was moved to Las Vegas in 2041 helped motivate the people of Nevada to intensify their state government's official historical research programs, an effort that continues to this day.

Nevada's Capitol had been moved due to budget concerns, motivated in large part by the fact that Southern Nevada's population swelled to over 5 million people. At the same time, the Reno—and Carson City—area's population remained stagnant due primarily to a saturation in buildable space, coupled by the fact water supplies dried up due to global waning that cause a 25-year drought that began in 2012-coupled, of course, by the ravages of World War III, which pretty much obliterated the north central part of the state from 1925-1929, a radioactive fallout zone that killed 1.6 million people in area encompassing Winnemucca and Elko in northern Nevada, clear to the Boise area. I mention this, because the nuclear-fallout zone had a negative impact on my staffs initial research in Mister Ballard's history more than a half century later. Thankfully, that 468,000-square-mile area was the only zone west of the Mississippi to get ravaged by nuclear fallout, while-as many of us know-six distinct zones in the east got hit, killing an estimated 23 million Americans.

Nearly five decades after the end of World War III, I attended the University of Nevada in Reno (UNR), even though that institution's prestige and student population had fallen off sharply. It seems college administrators there were so desperate for students that they even granted a full-ride scholarship to me, although I had been nothing better than a C-student in high school. I suppose the only thing that really sparked their interest in me was the fact that despite my lackluster grades, I had somehow managed to gain a reputation as a dogged researcher and a thoroughly intense questioner, always insisting on getting the facts straight. While these attributes might seem a lame-brained reason to present me with a scholarship, from their perspective I was the kind of person who eventually would help give their institution much-needed recognition.

Now, I'll have to say I honestly believe that they were "right." Even before the printing of this pamphlet and e-book, the controversy and intense publicity from this Ballard case alone has given UNR plenty of attention whether it's want or not. More than that, though, the Ballard Case, as it has come to be known, has resulted in just as much publicity for the university's mathematics department-the reasons of which we'll delve into later.

Much of what you'll discover involves Humboldt County High School in Winnemucca, Nevada, a former isolated railroad, mining, and agricultural community in the north-central part of the state that is now a ghost town within the nuclear fallout zone.

Misconceptions about the poem's origin had been perpetuated by a blockbuster movie released just three years ago in 2095. "Looking Back," still a runaway bestseller in Virtual-Digital Sales, stars Opie Russell, great-great-grandson of the late legendary actor Kurt Russell. In this movie, produced and released by Warner Bros.-Universal Pictures, Opie Russell plays the title role of Wes Ballard. In this film, which drew international acclaim and resulted in a best actor Oscar for Opie Russell, the title character of Wes Ballard writes the poem for his girlfriend, Wilhelmina Perry, while they both attended high school in Winnemucca in the spring of 1950. Played by Jennie Bowlander, the Wilhelmina character breaks her neck in a fall from her horse, Target, while in a barrel racing competition at the Humboldt County Fair.

As Wilhelmina lay near-dying in the Humboldt County Hospital, Ballard writes his fallen lover many dozens of love poems including the classic "Looking Back." These poems gradually motivate Wilhelmina to recover-and eventually to walk again.

Through that ordeal, young Wes Ballard managed to pay for the bulk of her medical expenses. Wes used most funds he earned working three different jobs.

Yet on April 13, 1950, the day Wilhelmina was to be released for a final time from the hospital after numerous operations-at least in this movie version-Wes Ballard was killed while driving there in a tragic auto accident on highway 40 near Winnemucca. For this movie, marketed as a "true" story, words from the actual poem penned by Wes Ballard, "Looking Back," had been incorporated into the film's title song, which became an instant Number-One hit in Cyber-Sound worldwide, breaking all sales records.

Needless to say, the film increased the legend of Wes Ballard. Before the movie's release, the Warner Bros-Universal press kit mentioned matter-of-factly that Wes Ballard had written the poem, which gained widespread acclaim by the 2030s.

Popular screenwriter Duane Nelson, himself a winner of five Oscars, was said to have based his work for this film on actual historical accounts of the poem-primarily from articles published in the Reno Gazette-Journal Cyber-Net Site from Oct. 3-18, 2037.

In fact, in perpetuating what I later determined was the "myth" that Wes Ballard had written this poem, upon the movie's release the screenwriter and actor appeared on major TV programs to pitch their film-including "Good Morning America-Today" on ABC-NBC, and even "True History," hosted by George Bush, great-great-grandson of former U.S. President George Herbert Walker Bush, the father of President George W. Bush. On these programs, as my office staff and I have since proven, Opie Russell and Duane Nelson perpetuated a horrible myth, dispelling the truth of the true nature and beginnings of the "Looking Back" poem for their own profit and personal gain.

Yet, from all the details that have been dug up since then, I must honestly conclude that I don't blame Russell or Nelson whatsoever. They had been led to believe these numerous mistruths, primarily due to erroneous news reports on the poem during the 1930s, which was followed by the blockbuster book, "Wes Ballard: The Truth & The Myth," at the time a runaway bestseller published in 2048 by Double-Day/Pocket Books, and written by Marcus Melton, grandson of the acclaimed Nevada author Wayne Rollan Melton-who himself was the son of internationally known newspaper executive and newspaper columnist Rollan Melton, who died of congestive heart failure in 2002. Wayne Melton, who died of Alzheimer's in 2036 at age 80, had instilled in his own son, Isaac, and grandson Marcus, the need for accuracy in their journalistic reports.

Be that as it may, I've concluded beyond a reasonable doubt that book author Marcus Melton failed miserably, by perpetuating many mistruths in "Wes Ballard: The Truth & The Myth." Now, none of the many mistakes from that book, and the eventual movie, could have ever been dispelled, if I had not received a single phone call on May 3, 2095, at 4:31 in the afternoon.

It was just one of an average four dozen similar phone calls received by myself and my staff on a typical weekday, each query with a different question or involving a specific topic. At the State Archives Office, we're paid to know-or to find out for certain-a wide variety of specific details on Nevada history. Many of these calls come from miners, hunting down specifics on what was found in old claims, or genealogists scouring for specifics on people who lived or worked in the Silver State. And a small percentage of queries come from students in high school and at the college level, many at Silver State University, formerly known as the University of Nevada Las Vegas.

Anyway, I happened to answer this particular call, primarily because my office personnel were swamped at the time, so without any hesitation I picked up the phone. It was Annie Johns, a senior at Las Vegas' Western High School, calling to ask for specifics on the Ballard automobile crash, so she could use those details in a paper she was writing for her history class. Without missing a beat, I immediately suggested to Annie that she simply get herself a copy of "Wes Ballard: The Truth & The Myth," since that particular publication surely would feature all blow-by-blow details of the accident. Just as quickly, Miss Johns let me know under no uncertain terms that she had scoured the book several times, and that there was not a single mention on specifics of the crash, only that the "car rolled several times, as it spun off the freeway. Wes was killed instantly."

Intrigued, and somewhat stunned by the author's oversight, I immediately used my office computer to punch up the Nevada Highway Patrol CyberSheet. As most of us know today, this system is a vast improvement from the former Internet communications systems, which were phased out in 2038, nearly a decade after World War III, and gradually replaced by the various systems that we enjoy today. Unlike the Internet, which for the most part was limited to Web pages and direct communications, the CyberSheet system instantly analyzes trillions of pieces of data, including information taken directly from the archives of government data storage systems.

Right away, this message popped onto my computer screen: "Information incomplete on Wes Ballard auto accident. Data obliterated or eliminated from data systems, due to nuclear fallout and bombings that destroyed state computer information systems in the Winnemucca, Nevada, area during World War III. . . .

Suggested other sources for information: Nevada State Historical Society, Hard-Copies Division, 2348 N. Mizpah Drive, Las Vegas, Nevada." Surprised to find this result, and even a bit upset with myself for forgetting that the Great War would have resulted in this obvious conclusion, I read the computer screen report to Annie-word-for-word-over the phone. Yet this young woman, whom I've since concluded is quite crafty and a firecracker of a researcher, informed me right away that she had already tried that route with no success. "The data is chock full of old paper-based reports, since double copies of each citation or investigation had been filed-at least through the late 1900s-in both Winnemucca, and in Las Vegas," Annie told me, sounding more like a 30-year-old barrister than a girl who would soon be graduating from high school. "I scoured every record there, and there was no mention of any citations or accident reports by anyone with the surname of Ballard, except for a driving permit issued to a Virgil B. Ballard, and one speeding ticket given to a guy named Joaquin Ballard. I don't know if any of these guys were related."

Intrigued, I found myself unable to suggest any short-term solution to Annie. She had already done all that could reasonably be expected of any average high school student, in getting basic details for a required homework assignment. Well, since I always take great pride in my job, even though-like I say, I hate the position with a dread-I told Annie merely that "we'll look into it, and get back to you." She politely said "thank you," adding that she looked forward to getting an answer because her paper was due in several days.

"What is it, boss? What's wrong?" Beverly asked, as soon as I clicked off my phone. "You look almost as if you've just received the most difficult question of your life."

"Haven't I told you, Bev, all questions are stupid?" I stood up and walked out my door. "For heaven's sakes, I think I just got a stupid question that might signal that one of the biggest frauds in Nevada history has been perpetuated on the people of the world."

"A fraud," Beverly followed me toward the office door. "What do you mean?"

"That famous poem, 'Looking Back.' It seems there's no accurate record on how its author was killed. You know the case-the poem, the book, the movie-all that?" "Sure. Who doesn't?"

"I'm confident we can straighten all this up. Hopefully, this will be just another quick check, maybe the subject of my next short article on Silver State Myths for 'Nevada Magazine.'"

Fully believing everything I had just said, I then took the short 5-minute SkyTube ride from Las Vegas to Carson City, Nevada. I jettisoned from the tube a half block from my home, which is on Washington Street, just five houses down from the former Nevada Governor's Mansion. Although this 448-mile one-way commute takes less than 10 minutes, I enjoy it, watching the expansive Nevada desert far below.

Eleven minutes after strolling from my office, I walked up the front steps of my small Tudor-style home. At the front door, my wife, Carolina, greeted me. Just inside the front door, we gave each other a long, warm, tight hug.

Carolina was dying of skin cancer.

"I'm so glad you're home," Carolina said.

"Me, too," I answered, while walking with her arm-in-arm to the living room couch. As I gently helped Carolina into a sitting position on her favorite chair, I began to think of my old high school girlfriend-Patty Carnahan, of how much I missed her. While I adore Carolina, and enjoy her companionship, not a day has passed when I haven't thought-at least briefly-of Patty. Momentarily, another thought crossed my mind, about that query I had received 15 minutes before, about Wes Ballard's fatal auto crash.

"I'll find the answer," I mumbled, while getting a blanket for Carolina, to make her comfortable.

"What was that?" Carolina asked.

"Nothing. Oh, nothing," I told my wife, actually thinking at that moment of how I wanted to get an accurate answer to Annie John's question. I'm just that kind of guy, a perennial professional.

CHAPTER TWO

By 9:15 that evening, I had put poor Carolina down for the night in our bed. As had been the pattern the previous several weeks, she began to softly moan in pain, till a healthy dose of medication finally took hold. For the past few days, the medicines seemed to be taking far less effect, and my senses told me it would be less than three months before life would end for my wife.

Glad to finally have some time for peace, quiet and reflection of my own, once she fell asleep for the night, I opened up a file that I had brought home on Annie Johns' query about the Ballard wreck. I opened the file and studied a State Archives Office Form I had filled out that afternoon, when speaking with her by phone. Little did I know at that moment, while sitting in my living room chair and petting my cat, Carlos, that Ballard Poem File-as it would come to be known-would swell during the following year later to 14 full wooden crates, jam packed detailed papers and old computer storage files.

For the moment though, as the hit Cyber-TV show "Boogies" came on my three dimensional living room screen, I had no reason to sense that this case would take more than a day to resolve. Quickly bored with the predictable "Boogies" program, which featured realistic scenes of monkeys mud-wrestling human game show contestants, I used my VoiceDemand remote to flip the screen into a Cyber-Book mode. "Change for reading," I said, glad this device at least takes orders better than some folks on my office staff.

Lickety-split, I had that best-selling book by Marcus Melton, "Wes Ballard: The Truth & Myth" on screen, from my personal archives. You see, I had purchased this book more than a quarter century earlier, way back while I attended the University of Nevada, in Reno. As far as I can recall, I had bought it in an effort to help quench my insatiable thirst for knowledge of Silver State history-especially rural areas.

Lots of people contend I possess a legendary ability to vividly recall intricate facts, in some cases many decades after I read a book or paper, or have a conversation. But for the life of me, at that moment while reviewing the old Melton book, I had little memory of these details that I began reading. Perhaps my widely known brainpower was finally slipping. Rather than ponder the matter, I scooped Carols the cat off my lap onto the floor. He always seems to get in the way, just about the time I'm making some discovery during my home-based research-getting in the way of one of the few things that make me happy, discovering interesting facts about the past.

While flipping through the book's first several pages, reviewing the table of contents I recalled hearing my college history professor,

Ben Crowley, recommend this book. The instructor insisted that the 278-page publication was a "mighty good read," largely because it dealt with intricacies of family life in north central Nevada in the mid-1900s-not to mention what seemed to be a thorough, in-depth recount of Wes Ballard's heroics when competing in rodeo arenas across the West in the late 1940s.

Sure enough, all those many years later, this time I found the book probably just as compelling as I had before. Only this time, pressed for time, and wanting only specific details. Details flashed before my eyes while cruising from screen to screen. I soon found myself, magnetized by the compelling context, a story of a hard-working teen-age boy who lived a simple, good and honest life.

Then, finally, on page 17, below a picture purported to be Wes Ballard as he received a "First Prize" ribbon for winning a major rodeo competition in his junior year at Humboldt County High School, was that now-world-famous poem, "Looking Back," credited to him.

> Sweet is the opium of idle thought
> And an addict loves his dream
> But when one so young has come so soon
> To the age of reminiscence
> It shows a life that has passed its goal
> And now the pipe of I did, not I will.

As Carlos attempted unsuccessfully to jump back on my lap, I gently brushed him away, and without missing a beat I read and reread those lines penned long ago by a young Wes Ballard. What insightful words, what wisdom's, to have come from one so youthful-of such a tender age. And somehow, at that moment, I thought of the actual Wes Ballard, and in that very moment I knew that I would have enjoyed meeting him-even though he happened to enjoy horses, perhaps my least favorite animal.

Both intrigued and mesmerized by this story, I flipped to the photo section. My favorites were those of Wes and his girlfriend, Jennie Bowlander, standing arm-in-arm at a picnic a year or two before her critical injury from the horse riding accident. As I looked at them, I found myself gazing at the delighted, seemingly luminescent expressions in both their faces. From this perspective, it seemed to me as if this young couple, tender in years-children, really-felt as if the whole world and its many bright possibilities lay before them. Little did they know of the tragedies that would strike each of them, within six years of that delightful afternoon.

In the background, a ways behind the couple, I noticed an unidentified man who wore a military uniform. The man in the uniform seemed sad, almost morose, as if he had just returned from battlefields. And oddly, everyone else in the background area beamed in happiness, as if they shared the same delightful feelings as the love-struck youngsters. Intrigued, I zoomed in to enlarge the image of the soldier many times. A close inspection confirmed that the soldier maintained a pained expression, not as if he was jealous of the young couple-but almost as if there was an inner sadness about him. Always one to get as much detail as possible, I zoomed the image even more-to the maximum of what my Cyber-Book would allow. Then, I saw a name, bold and distinct, in white lettering embossed on a standard black military-style template: "Virgil B. Ballard." Increasingly curious, I flipped through the book to find any mention of this gentleman. A few pages confirmed that this was the only brother of Wes Ballard, nine years his senior. At least that's what I calculated Virgil's age to be, judging by various references and inferences, things I concluded from various details in the book. Yet despite intricate info given on Wes Ballard, including thorough recounts of his many rodeo victories, of his bravery in saving a young child from a burning home, and of his romance with Jennie, little was said about Virgil B. Ballard.

In a flash, of course, I recalled that during my check of highway patrol records, earlier that afternoon I had learned that a man by that name had been issued a driving permit in the Winnemucca community. And now that I knew this was Wes' brother, I found it interesting-and I resolved, then and there, that someday I would at least make a brief mention of Virgil B. Ballard, in one of my future columns on Nevada history. Anyway, I found the book's brief section on the car wreck, and realized that the high school student Annie Johns had been right-there was no detail.

With little need for reflection, I found that oversight rather odd, especially since Marcus Melton had been thorough in the rest of the book-in almost every respect. My memory began to fail me for once here, for right away I began to realize that the reference to the "wreck" in this book had been the first ever account I could ever remember of the accident. Melton's recount failed to quote a single source in relation to the wreck, and there was no mention whatsoever of any Highway Patrol report. This, certainly, would prove especially difficult for me to overcome, since that division of state government had been shut down for good in 2021—the year gasoline-powered automobiles finally were abolished in the United States, partly because there was no need for such contraptions anymore.

"Computer, record my words," I said, confident my home electronics unit would do its job well-although it had sustained some power-related malfunctions the previous year. "Here is a reminder to myself to visit the Nevada Historical Society, for details on any Highway Patrol reports from that region and era, and . . ."

Just then, the usual "buzz-buzz" echoed in my ear, the signal that someone was trying to call me on my implanted earphone. Usually, especially while at home, I just ignore the thing and let answer in "record" mode. I detest the notion of anyone being allowed to bother me or anyone else whenever they choose. Thankfully, people have an option to ignore their earphones. This isn't like the old days, the era of Wes Ballard and well beyond that, where people had actual phones in their homes and offices-devices that in many cases weighed up to a pound or even more. Like most people, I suppose, I haven't had any problem at all with my earphone since it was implanted when I was three days old. The only hassle with it since being an infant, at least for me, has been trying to get the blasted number change-so that people from much earlier in life wouldn't be able to call me on a mere whim.

Anyway, this time my senses told me it might be a good idea to answer. "Hello, this is Ben Rivera." It couldn't have been more than a millisecond before a young female voice announced blatantly: "Mister Rivera, I'm mad at you." Stunned, partly since I failed to recognize the voice, I immediately grew testy. "Who is this?" I asked. "Why are you calling at this time of night? How did you get my Ear-Number?" After what seemed like a lengthy pause, enough time for me to make a Protein Sandwich, the voice shot back: "You mislead me, when I spoke to you this afternoon."

"What are you talking about? Who is this? Is this Annie? Annie Johns, is this you?" Once again, there was another pause. Finally, she spoke up: "Yes, this is Annie. I didn't mean for you to get angry at me like this, sir. But you should have told me that Wes Ballard's car hit a truck head-on. You should have known that."

"What? A truck," I grew perplexed, and I'll have to admit I usually like feisty, vocal people like Annie who deal with my office-since they help make life a challenge. "I haven't seen or heard any record of a truck being on the highway? Where did you find out about that, young woman? And why are you mad at me in the first place if I didn't happen to know that fact? What's the big deal?" "The big deal is, you're supposed to be the state's premiere expert in historical questions-and you didn't even have an answer," Annie said. "You shouldn't even have your job, sir, if it takes a high school student like me to find the answers for you."

"Well, I . . ." and then, before I could get a word in, my earphone line went dead. Obviously, this teen dynamo had hung up. I pushed the instant redial button, now angry at myself and determined to speak with her. But then something strange happened, for instead of getting a ring I got a "buzzzzzzz" sound that lasted maybe 10 seconds, followed by a recording: "there is no such number, as that which you have dialed."

Perplexed, I said "hang-up, hang-up," which is the earphone's signal to do just that. But this is the first time in my life, using this same device all those years, that it hasn't managed to punch-ring through to whoever initially called me-except for those using a "caller ID block mode," which this was not. While many people are unable to do that with their earphones, mine has never had such a blocking feature-for, since childhood, my dad managed to help get me high-priority info clearance.

Off kilter due to this unwanted interruption, I stood and walked into the kitchen and opened the Solo-Arctic for a glass of cold Zebra-Protein Juice. I began wondering whether to let the entire auto accident question drop, since it seemed at this point there obviously was no need-since Annie had determined that Wes

Ballard's vehicle had hit a truck. Even if that was the case, though, the public didn't know it-all everyone assumed is that the car merely veered off the road and overturned.

As State Archivist, it's my job to ensure that such inaccuracies-if, indeed, that happens to be the case-don't get perpetuated in the media, and in local legend for that matter. If, indeed, the car had hit a truck, the public would need to know. This would be necessary as soon as possible as far as I was concerned, since there's almost nothing worse than a gullible public uses incorrect information in making its opinions on major issues.

Before long, I put on my anti-bacterial plastic pajamas, and curled up into bed beside Carolina, nestling up to her to warm her back. Usually not the kind of guy who gets upset about work-related matters, and never prone to bring such problems into the home environment, I mysteriously found myself tossing and turning. I failed to get those phone calls from Annie out of my head, and the nagging question of how Wes Ballard was killed kept gnawing at my brain-like a pit bull that has latched onto a chicken.

Awake, lying on my back, and staring at the ceiling, I took a deep breath and realized why this particular case was so important to me, why it poked at my heart. Everything came down to Wes Ballard and especially his poem "looking back" which is among the few major, undying legends in state history. I knew I would become the focus of ridicule for generations to come, should I ever knowingly allow a major mistruth about such a premiere legend to perpetuate-without trying to resolve the situation.

Like I say, I'm usually a laid-back, easygoing fellow for the most part. But this worry kept me awake till well past 2 in the morning. Little did I know at the time that there would be many sleepless nights for me during the coming year, during which time I would be-unwillingly and gradually-losing a whopping 100 pounds, gnawed with worry, and heartache, and the subject of public ridicule. Through it all, I thought this anguish would end, and that I'd find happiness, if I could only get at the truth.

CHAPTER THREE

Despite my restless night, I awakened feeling refreshed and alive, ready to "attack" the day, at 5:05 on the morning of May 4. A full 45 minutes before sunrise, I popped into the shower and was out the door at 5:30-greeting hospice volunteer Sheila Morgan, as she arrived to spend the morning with Carolina.

"Enjoyed your article in the paper this morning, Ben, about the demolition of the Mirage Hotel in 2047," Sheila said, as we passed each other on the front walkway. "Fascinating stuff. What will you come up with next?"

"Oh, I have a few surprises up my sleeve, I hope," I said, admiring her fiery attitude. "Oh, by the way, could you check on Carolina's pain medication-it doesn't seem to be working at all."

"Sure thing," Sheila said. "Did you know you forgot to put your pants on this morning?"

Stunned as I stood on the front sidewalk, I realized that this woman wasn't joking. I dashed toward the front door, perhaps faster than an Olympian, threw on my trousers and gave poor Carolina another quick peck goodbye. Back out the front door in a flash, I strolled the half block to the SkyTube. Usually, after pressing the red "take me," button, I have no more than 15 seconds for a fresh tube to arrive. This time, though, it didn't even approach after a full five minutes, and there wasn't even that usual "swoosh" sound that signals it's arrival. Of course, everyone knows that each tube has just enough room for one person to crawl inside. Well, within six or seven minutes after I got there, at least 15 of my neighbors were lined up behind me, each waiting for his or her turn at a fresh SkyTube. Billy Owen, my neighbor to the south of me, a hydrologist from Oak Park, Illinois, said he was going home there for breakfast-and that his mother expected him to arrive in about 10 minutes. Most others in line, without evening having to tell me-since I'm familiar with their usual routes-were headed for their workplaces mostly in cities across the West including Los Angeles, Seattle, San Francisco, Salt Lake City, and even Reno-which now adjoins Carson City, but once was 30 miles to the north, in the days before its monster-sized expansion.

"Hi, Ben, are you going to make it to this afternoon's Reno luncheon, honoring Realtors® from the past?" asked another neighbor, Monica Sloan. "We'd sure love to have you there, maybe you could make a few remarks about the history of real estate in our community."

"You know, I might do that," I answered, honestly, just as the tube finally arrived, a full 15 minutes after I first pushed the button. I stepped inside, but made sure to make a cordial goodbye. "I don't remember this contraption taking anywhere near this long.

See ya, and feel free to call me to let me know if you can get me a ticket."

Three minutes later, while en route to my office and about halfway to Las Vegas, somewhere over the Tonopah area, I decided to take another route and visit Western High School instead. I needed to see that feisty little creature Annie Johns, and meet her for myself. If that little punk had the nerve to call me and bother me at home, then for all intents and purposes I had every right to see her at her school. Immediately upon my arrival on campus, I reported to the principal's office, since that's the appropriate and required protocol in such instances. Since state officials such as myself have the legal power to see citizens wherever and whenever we want, I felt comfortable knowing she wouldn't be able to escape my inquiries.

"There is no such student at this school," principal Justin Ericson told me. "And she told you her name is Annie Johns?"

Once I confirmed that, Justin put the info into his office DataScreen, and immediately determined there is no such student by that name in the entire school district. He then punched the name into the Human-Database, instantly determining that there are 18,342 people by that name who live West of the Mississippi River.

Of those, 1,479 are between ages 16 and 19, which seemed about the right age we should hunt for-at least to me-since I could swear her voice was that of a person in that age range.

"Shows here that 26 young women within that demographic category and name live or work in the Las Vegas area," Justin said. "Too many to pin down the right one, in less than a minute."

"I have an idea," I said right away. "Let me play a recording of my phone conversation I had with her last night. We'll have

Voice-Recognition handle it." Right away, I played a small portion of the conversation, allowing the sounds to go directly into Justin's computer speakerphone.

"We have an instant 'hit,'" Justin said. "That's her name all right. The computer says she's Annie May Johns, who attended this school two years ago but dropped out before graduation. She's 19 years old now, and she'll turn 20 next week. She was born May 10, 2078, in San Diego. Do you want to know where she is now, Ben?"

"You bet I want to speak with her, that little bitch," I had to let it out, and I felt comfortable telling this to Justin, since we knew each other from out days as university classmates in Reno. "A compute satellite scan finds her at this very moment in the 5700 block of North Las Vegas Boulevard, walking toward the entrance to the former Luxor Hotel."

"Sounds like she works there," I said, while taking an instant computer printout of Annie's mug shot from a printer adjoining Justin's computer. "I'm going over there right away to talk with this gal."

I then took the one-minute walk to the nearest SkyTube, popped inside, spoke the coordinates and got to the front entrance of the former Luxor within two minutes after determining Annie's identity and whereabouts. As I opened the hotel front door, Justin Ear-Phoned me with an update on this woman, her work background and family data. Thankfully, at least from my perspective, satellites had been able to track her exact location, beaming in on microchips that the government requires be installed into the skin of each American less than one hour after birth. I walked through the front lobby, as Justin informed me that Annie currently had a job in this same building, working as a maid.

Of course, Las Vegas' gambling economy virtually disappeared in 2015 amid a surge in Internet gambling, which was later surpassed in the 2070s by CyberGambling. Despite the change, southern Nevada still managed to thrive as a major destination and vacation resort, thanks to its energizing weather-coupled with the fact that many of the original hotel structures had been preserved.

"Annie May Johns, I'd like to have a word with you," I told this young woman, under no uncertain terms, the moment I saw her carrying a water bucket as she opened the door to an employee service room adjoining the hotel lobby. "You have harassed me, a state official, and you should know that doing that is a crime."

"I was wondering how stupid you were, how long it would take you to find me and show up here to question me," she said, not acting surprised at all. "What is it with you bureaucrat types, where you think you're so much smarter than other people?" "Young woman, giving incorrect information to a public official such as myself is a felony, I hope you know that," I said, leaning up against a wall near her. "I could have you hauled down and locked up in Absolute Lock-Up for a few years, unless you cooperate. I'm in a mood to do just that right now, unless you come clean." "Mister Rivera, you're talking mighty tough for a wimp," she said, setting her water bucket down on the floor and using a finger-print code to open the door.

"I'm highly familiar with your career history, sir, and I know you haven't come even close to doing that to anyone during your quarter century of government service."

"You think you're cool, don't you?" I pressed her, not enjoying this conversation at all. "I could just forget you, Miss Johns, and walk away from here right now. After all, no one was physically injured. But you must realize that what you did was significant, because you're toying with a major part of Nevada history."

"You're damn right, the Ballard family is important to this state-I should know, because . . ." She grinned as she said this, while pushing the door open . . . . "Because, I, uh . . . . Because my . . ."

"Out with it. You're wasting my time . . ."

"You see, my great-great-great-grandmother knew Wes Ballard's brother."

"So?"

"If I tried to explain it to you, sir, you wouldn't understand."

"Sounds to me like you're just trying to play games. You're not giving solid detail," I started getting angry, primarily due to the fact I get frustrated when people have a difficult time explaining basic facts in a short period. "Mister Rivera, if I told you everything I know about this, the family legends that have been passed down to me through the generations, even if I gave you the truth-every detail-you'd accuse me of lying."

"Let's cut to the chase," I said, while accompanying her inside the workroom. There, she immediately started putting laundry into washing machines. "If you're one of them, a true descendant of someone who knew the Ballards, then why in the world did you call up with that lame-brained question about not knowing how the wreck originally happened-and then calling back with the hit-the-truck tale, and-certainly, lying about being a student at Western High."

"Everything is true, I just . . ."

"Girl, you sound more like a flake, a certified nut-case, than a common criminal who needs to be in jail," I said, actually helping her stuff laundry into washing machines. "You better come clean fast, or I'm calling a Lock-Up Cop." With this, the young woman started balling her head off. As she wept, tears rolling in rivers down her red cheeks, I admired her long blond hair and the appearance of her curvaceous body, good enough-I'm sure-for her to have been one of Las Vegas most titillating showgirls, had she been born a full 100 years ago. At that moment, if I had been a young and single gentleman, I would have cradled my arms lovingly around her, showing genuine sympathy and understanding. All my senses, ever fiber of my intuition, told me Annie was a woman who needed to be cared for by a strong yet sensitive man. She's the kind of gal that when average American guys first see her, they think of "sex," without them realizing her male-female relationships require much more mental intimacy.

"Forgive me, Annie, maybe I was a little too rough on you." I wanted to hug her, to do something-anything, for I'm never so cruel and heartless. "Please, try to calm down, so we can talk about this with level heads."

Annie continued weeping unabated, so intensely that I figured there could be no way to get her back to her senses. Then, after about one minute, she suddenly calmed herself, and stood straight, putting her hands through her own hair as if to put herself back together.

"I never cry, never," Annie said. "I've just been thinking about all this so much, that I've had everything pent up inside me."

"It may seem to you, Miss Johns, that I behave like some sort of insensitive monster. I'm not that kind of guy."

"I think you better leave now, sir," she started turning on laundry machines. "I made a mistake in calling you, because you'll never understand what I try to tell you, and you'd never be able to ferret out all the actual details anyway."

"Test me."

"I'm going to get fired if I spend all my time here talking to you. I have work to do."

"What time does your shift end, I could pick you up here then."

"Let's never see each other again. Please forget that I ever called you."

Persistent, I then made a brief but emphatic, detailed and passionate speech to this young woman, telling her of the importance of the Ballard family history to our state. Annie seemed attentive, as if she would remember my every word for the rest of her life.

"Okay, okay," she finally said. "Today, I have a short shift. Pick me up here at noon. I want to take you somewhere. I want you to see something that may spark your interest."

CHAPTER FOUR

Numbed by the experience, I returned to my office, where I went to my own desk and sat back in my chair. A lengthy quiet time, a period of gentle, thoughtful reflection, never hurts anyone in such situations as far as I'm concerned. I needed to be able to think clearly, to put this all in perspective. Something deep inside told me that I was onto something big, but I wasn't quite sure what that might be. I gazed out my office window, toward the rolling hills of Red Rock Canyon, far off in the distance. I wiped a huge puddle of perspiration from my forehead, aware that the conflict with Annie had made me far hotter than I first realized. Sensing a need for solitude, I turned up the magnetism on my office window, a technology that allows the canyon to come into full five from 15 miles away-blocking out, virtually obliterating any view of those many thousands of structures that are between here and there.

Just as I finally started to relax, my earphone rang, and it was Sheila Morgan, the hospice worker who cares for Carolina three mornings a week. "It's bad today, Ben. Your wife is in the worst condition I've seen her in so far." Understandably upset, I asked Sheila to do everything she could to make my wife as comfortable as possible. From our earlier conversations, we knew that within the next few weeks I would start a leave of absence, to stay home with my wife until the end. The sad thing is, that just six months earlier, poor Carolina had missed out by just one point-one lousy, stinking point-in the Annual United States Life Lottery. Almost everyone knows that's the process where our government must decide who with terminal illnesses gets to live or die. Of course, breast cancer was "cured" for good in 2022, and for the next three decades that technology saved many millions of lives worldwide-too many lives. If everyone who got terminally ill were cured, then the world population would swell beyond its capacity. Sadly, people must die naturally, so that others might live. That's why our government, in cooperation with other nations of the world, holds the annual lottery. A full 22 percent of those with terminal illnesses of many kinds in the United States are allowed to live, to receive the inevitable cures that will enable them to live for many years to come.

Needless to say, then, Carolina and I awaited last year's lottery with both anticipation and trepidation. And when she "lost," during the national drawing of those despicable number balls, she kept a straight face-accepting her doom with dignity. It was I who lost my senses, weeping for several days, the first time I've cried like that since half of my beloved hometown of San Francisco was submerged in the rising oceans in 2080-destroying my childhood home, and leaving my parents destitute.

By this point, though, the morning of that phone call from Sheila, I had managed to steel myself so to speak, mentally and physically-I hoped-prepared to handle the inevitable ravages of Mother Nature's insistent nagging and cruelty. In the face of all my efforts to gain happiness and to show a cheery face, deep inside I had been crushed.

Yet managing to focus on the work at hand, I pushed the intercom and summoned my best investigator, Ruby Sanders, into my office. Ruby and I have always had difficulty getting along with each other, primarily because we hold vastly different philosophies about the meanings and purposes of life. Ruby thinks of each human being as a blessing, and that his or her naturally curious mind is a wonderful biological machine. From Ruby's perspective, the brain will enable people everywhere to find answers to all major problems. Holding a much opposite perspective, convinced people have screwed things up as much as is humanly possible, I gave up on arguing with Ruby about all this years ago. Be that as it may, we always somehow manage to tolerate each other, perhaps out of a mutual desire for professionalism.

"Ruby, I need your help. Can you do a background search, a little family history on Annie Johns, born May 10, 2078, in San Diego."

"Sounds easy enough," Ruby said, using her typical robot-like voice. "I don't know why you need to use me on something so basic as this. I should have an answer for you within a few minutes."

As soon as Ruby walked out of my office, I remembered my promise to my Carson City neighbor, Monica Sloan, that I would try to attend this afternoon's Realtors® luncheon up in Reno. I phoned Monica, and told her there was little chance I would be able to make the session, but even so I asked her to please keep a seat available for me anyway. I didn't know how long my noon session with Annie would take. With any luck, my conversation with the young woman would take no more than a half hour, allowing me enough time to visit the last few minutes of the real estate industry gathering.

"Here's the report, Ben. It looks like basic stuff to me," Ruby surmised, as she handed over the instant file on Annie John's basic family history. Sure enough, Annie Johns is the great-great-granddaughter of Holly Ann Saunders Johns, who was born Dec. 13, 1960, at Cottonwood Maternity Hospital, in Murray Utah, between Salt Lake City and Sandy.

"Please find out everything you can about this woman, this Holly person, because I think she may have known the brother of Wes Ballard."

"That doesn't sound like any big deal to me," Ruby used her usual gruff voice, which she only has when chatting with me. With other people, Ruby's tone always echoes sweet and cheery. "I've got plenty of important work to do, rather than chase down . . ."

"Ruby, you're always such a firecracker, a delight when you whine this way," I said, trying to diffuse the situation. Although she's my best researcher, she always needs a little smoothing out in order to get her on track. "These details, whatever you find, I can use for my research on Wes Ballard's brother. I think it might make an interesting topic for my next column, just a few basics anyway on the 'unknown brother.'"

Ruby grumbled non-stop as she left the room, a sure sign to me that she actually liked the idea of this brief assignment. Ruby never admitted it, but she always shines at her work, especially on any task that's likely to get ample public attention.

"Though I've got plenty of more important things to do, I should have a little something for you-I hope-by late this afternoon," she said, gently closing the door behind her. If Ruby had her way, though, I know she would prefer to slam it as hard as possible.

Since I'm the boss, and because I can spend my work time doing pretty much whatever I want, I spent the next few hours doing computer research on Annie May Johns. Records at American Security Association, a privatized company that took over all duties of the former Social Security Administration, shows that she has worked a succession of odd-, low-paying jobs since she was 16 years old. And sure enough, she actually attends Western High School at night, not for that school's regular sessions, but for studies to obtain her General Diploma, formerly known as the General Education Degree or GED. Annie's father is Virgil Ballard Johns, great-grandson of Kristopher Johns, a son of Holly Ann Saunders Johns, the woman who apparently knew Virgil Ballard.

But why in the world, I wondered then, would one of Holly's distant relatives, nearly a century later, have the name given name of Virgil Ballard Johns. Was Holly married to Virgil Ballard, the brother of the famous poet? One thing seemed certain, in finding her dad's name, I had apparent-or at least possible-confirmation that at least a smattering of Annie May John's story might have at least some truth to it.

On schedule, I met Annie at noon at the back entrance to the Luxor. Right away I sensed she seemed more vibrant and energized than in the morning. She insisted we ride a golf-cart size device to her Foot-Wheels, which were parked about ten blocks away. This makes little sense to me, requiring people to park their Foot-Wheels so far from where they work, especially considering the fact Foot-Wheels are the same size, and shape as roller skates-used frequently in the 1900s and early this century. But, of course, as we all know every Foot-Wheel needs to be re-powered between uses. Energy conscious Luxor executives require that its employees park their Foot-Wheels in a public lot, in order to re-power on the public energy line.

"I hope you don't mind this extra inconvenience," Annie observed, as we pulled from the Luxor parking lot. "I want to take you somewhere that I know you will find interesting. A graveyard."

"A graveyard?"

"That's right," Annie said, popping a Sound-Tape into the radio tube. "Along the way to my Foot-Wheels, I think you'll enjoy listening to this old tape recording." Before I could ask her what it was, Annie turned up the volume, and right away we were listening to the voice of what obviously seemed to be an old man.

"I drove cattle from Texas, and various other points-that was 1898," the voice said, a rather formal yet somehow folksy tone prevailing. "I lived in no-man's land in the early 1890s, in what is now known as the Okalahoma Panhandle . . . ." Intrigued, I needed to get more details on this narrator, before hearing much more: "Annie, is this real. This is an old recording, of the actual guy?"

"Yes, it's Wes Ballard's grandfather, J.J. Ballard, you need to hear every word he says."

"This is JJ Ballard we're listening to!" I exclaimed, both awestruck and skeptical, since I knew full well that was the name of the noted poet Wes Ballard's grandfather.

Instinctively, I knew I needed to keep quiet and listen to every word possible, as Annie steered the cart. We went at such a slow speed, I knew it would take us at least 10 minutes to get to our destination.

"I worked for various cattle companies, till 1894, when I went to Woodward County, Oklahoma, at Beaver City, where I learned that claims for property were being accepted. As a young man, I staked my claim on a good piece of land, and from there set off to attend school in eastern Tennessee," he said, his vocal cadence methodical and rather predictable, yet somehow compelling as well. As the words flowed forth, I sat on the edge of my passenger seat, riveted by every word. I knew full well that if this recording were authentic, it would be a rare, valuable and seemingly priceless find. Such old-time recordings of actual Western pioneers were virtually impossible to track down, since any of them that existed had already been found and made public by this point.

"But it was wet, clammy, sticky weather there in Tennessee," the voice continued. "I had lost a good bit of my health while there because of this, and I ended up broke, sick, and discouraged. I settled down a bit in an attempt to regain health and fix my finances. It was then that I began to handle a good many small mules..."

Fixated on every word, I finally realized-momentarily-that we had arrived in the Foot-Wheels parking lot. Annie had put the cart into a "park" mode, but we sat there, together, motionless and listening. Like me, she sat riveted to the tape, as if she somehow needed to hear every word as well. And yet in a flash, giving it little thought, I realized she must have already listened to this many times-if, indeed, it was real.

"Well, as time passed, I began to do occasional business with a man known as Brigham Young, as a mail contractor," the voice of J.J. Ballard said in a matter-of-fact way. "In early 1900, I did some horse trading, and I traded with this Brigham Young, giving him a mule that was considered to be 'balky.'"

Behind us, the driver of another cart honked his horn, angry that we blocked his path. Mesmerized by this recording, though, I gave this interruption little thought.

"I got myself a wife in Texas, and brought her back to where I lived, and soon met again with that one gentleman named Brigham Young," the voice said. "By that time, he started calling me Brother Ballard, for reasons known only to him. And he started asking me every sort of question imaginable about everything having to do with myself. That's the kind of guy he was, Brigham Young needed to know everything."

Amazed, I sensed that this recording was indeed authentic, and that I had just-thanks to Annie's help-stumbled across a major find, one surely to get international attention. After all, Brigham Young was a founder of the Church of Jesus Christ of Latter Day Saints, which this century has grown by more than 1 billion members worldwide.

"Now, my own brother, Isaac, came to meet Brigham Young separately as a passenger on his stage line", J.J. Ballard continued, unabated. "On one occasion, my brother saw Mister Young being frustrated by a stubborn mule, that I had traded to him. And Brigham Young pointed this out to my brother, telling him: 'I often do business with JJ Ballard. We take turns getting the best of each other. Sometimes he gets the best of me, and sometimes I get the best of him. But in trading me this mule, he got the best of me.'

"My brother got a good, hearty laugh at hearing this, when Brigham Young suddenly pointed out that, 'Hey, you look like him.' After much nudging and encouragement, Isaac finally had to admit to Brigham Young that we were brothers."

Spellbound, I briefly noticed that the driver behind us was blaring his horn, almost non-stop, for we obviously were blocking him from his travels: "bleep-bleep-bleep." Undaunted and headstrong, I continued listening to the recording, while Annie May Johns finally got the message from behind us, and she began to cruise around the Foot-Wheels parking lot. I paid little or no attention to this development, because-at least for the moment-the recording of JJ Ballard had become just about the most important thing in the world to me.

"By this point, Brigham Young has passed to his reward. And I hope that wherever he is, he is not bothered by a balky mule," JJ Ballard proclaimed in that old-Western, folksy way that only a handful of actors are good at mimicking. Hearing this, I literally felt my heart flutter, since even more than a few minutes before I knew this recording was indeed one of the finds of the century. And I sense that every word of it was authentic.

"Nothing is more vicious or ferocious than a predatory wolf," JJ Ballard said, continuing on to explain the great damage wolves had inflected upon livestock through the old Western U.S. He then recounted the time he personally hunted down a wolf for many miles in Colorado and Wyoming, finally catching up with his prey thanks to a horse that had "good wind, about its only redeeming quality."

Ballard had finally cornered the varmint in a crevasse by a river. Terrified and completely exhausted, its body drenched in puddles of sweat, the trapped wolf growled at JJ Ballard, who was determined to slash the animal's throat with a knife. But in one last, heated attempt for survival, the wolf lunged forward and gnawed at the boot of the heroic if not downright foolhardy JJ Ballard. Using all the energy he could muster, Ballard knifed the wolf in a front leg, before jabbing at the throat. Within one month of that incident, the wolfs head had been mounted on a fireplace for all to see-a major trophy, indeed, for such creatures were both feared and hated with a dread.

"We'll listen to the rest later," Annie clicked off the radio and popped out the tape, while shifting the cart into park. The moment we stopped, a few people walked up to take the cart for themselves. That's to be expected, since the public, for short-term transportation, shares such devices. Anyway, in a second, Annie and I were standing beside her personal Foot-Wheels, which were parked into an electric outlet.

"Where on earth did you receive that recording?" I asked Annie, as she unhooked her Foot-Wheels from the power outlet.

"Oh, I received it from my great-grandfather, Kristopher Johns, who had received it from his own sister-Ashley," Annie proclaimed, as she hooked on her Foot-Wheels, securing them to her feet, and around super-long metal boots that went way past her knees and over her upper thighs-clear to her butt. Most people need at least a few minutes to strap their Foot-Wheels on, but right away I realized Annie possesses great athleticism, for it took her no more than 15 seconds.

"Where do you want to take me?" I inquired, while putting on a pair of Foot-Wheel Passenger Boots, which she had rented for a Dollar-MAX at a nearby dispenser machine.

"I already told you, the cemetery."

"Why there? And why should I trust you, young woman, considering your attitude?"

"You'll have to trust me," she said, clicking on her Foot-Wheels, and setting it onto a rail. Instinctively, I latched on behind Annie, and latched a metal double-hook from the crotch area of my Passenger Boots, through a hole-ring that protruded from the upper rear of her boots. I know this situation seems embarrassing to look at, and most of us have seen it, but that's simply the way these contraptions are built, and there's no getting around that. "Where is the cemetery?"

"It's in Reno."

"Reno! But that's 475 miles away! You're going to go that far on this? Why don't we just take a SkyTube? That would only take us about two minutes to get there." "Get this into your thick head, please, mister. I'm not rich-class, like you. I'm working class. Don't work yourself into a fuss. This thing will get us there in 15 minutes. A little slower, but good enough to do the job."

She clicked on the Foot-Wheel motor, and I heard it's gentle "hum," sounding more like that of a computer than an engine.

"Whose grave are we going to see?"

"We're going to the grave of Virgil Ballard . . . . Hang on for the ride."

CHAPTER FIVE

Annie's estimate of 15 minutes travel time meant we would be going at 1,900 miles per hour, super-slow by today's standards. Yet I knew full well that she obviously took this mode of transportation for the reason she gave, for financial reasons-or because she enjoyed going on what we commonly call the "open road." Like all other Foot-Wheel travelers, she would pay substantially less than SkyTube users, one Dollar-MAX per minute for a Foot-Wheel compared to 11 Dollar-Maxes for SkyTube use.

On the positive side, this meant we'd be able to travel by land, helping to give me a new perspective, although we'd be traveling far faster than the human mind can assimilate most details. Nonetheless, even though my job often takes me into rural Nevada for intense, in-depth research, I must confess that I rarely take this form of travel-maybe only once every three years or so. And even then, it's only because one of my associates insists. This time, at least I was traveling with someone I didn't know, which at least helped make the ride a bit interesting.

Rather than staring at Annie's curvaceous back along the way, which might seem a natural for a guy my age at 54, I allowed my senses to take full view of the high desert mountains, hills and valleys, as we blasted north on the former U.S. Highway 95, now known as Nevada FW-9, the "FW" standing for Foot-Wheel.

The roller-skate like contraption on Annie's Feet were hooked into a rail that's embedded into the former highway, which now is a rubberized surface to prevent injury.

In fact, it had only been about a week before this trip that I read in a popular national Cyber-Mag that there hasn't been a single driving-related injury-or even a death-on a Foot-Wheel in the past 48 years. That's quite a stunning record, especially when considering that there were many hundreds of annual highway fatalities-especially in rural areas-during those times before cars were banned. Thankfully, at least from the perspective of today's citizens, skies worldwide are picture-perfect-as clean as they were 10,000 years ago. The only remaining downside is this persistent ozone layer problem, a leftover environmental hazard from the era when mankind ravaged the earth.

"So, you say we're going to see the grave of Virgil Ballard?" I asked Annie, on a speaker system that connects our helmets-as we approached Tonopah, halfway between Las Vegas and Reno. She had temporarily slowed down to 300 miles per hour, as we zipped along the Foot-Wheel track above the community. "So Virgil, Wes Ballard's big brother, he's the guy your dad is named after."

"How in the world did you know that?" Annie acted surprised, as she punched it back up to 1,900 miles per hour the moment we finished getting through Tonopah. "You've been doing some checking into me, haven't you?" "It's my job," I said, glorifying at the sight of the next high-desert valley. "Who could blame me for doing a little background research beforehand. For all I know, you could be a serial killer, out to make me your next victim."

"If I was a serial killer, you wouldn't be my next victim. You would have been my first victim. I hope you take that the right way."

"Oh, boy, you are an angry gal, aren't you? I'm still trying to feel you out, so to speak-not that way, mind you. It's just that your personality is a little difficult to pin down."

"Stop worrying about me, mister, okay? I would like you to concentrate on your research, and forget about me as soon as you can."

"Fine."

At that point, my opinion on this gal kept vacillating, changing every 15 minutes or so. One minute I'd think of her as this sweet, delicious and enticing beauty that cares deeply for the world, and the next I'd make her out to be some sort of lunatic. One thing seemed sure, at least from my perspective, she seemed unhappy-almost as if she always strived for some sort of inner peace she never quite attained.

Momentarily, Reno came into view, the skyline void of any skyscrapers. All this city's former hotel-casino resorts had been taken down, razed using public money, after the live gambling industry fizzled. Quaint bungalows, art lofts and walkthrough country-style stores, reminiscent of the 1930s and 1940s in small-town America, and increasingly popular, had replaced those monstrosities. Anyway, Annie didn't even need to steer, as we cruised into town along the former Interstate, now called Nevada FW-2. A Foot-Wheel system requires a driver to punch in a destination before a journey begins. Computers take over from there, ensuring travel speeds are safe for road and weather conditions, while communicating with other Foot-Wheels in order to prevent them from colliding. Satellite systems handle much of the rest, continually monitoring a moving Foot-Wheel's path, in order to ensure it stops, slows or accelerates in order to avoid potential dangers.

Feeling safe and at ease, I feel glad we've taken this mode of transportation. I sighed, and took a deep breath, relaxed and at ease after we pulled off FW-2 onto Stoker Street. Within moments, we pull onto Cemetery Road. Just up ahead, I saw an Archway that said: "Mountain View Cemetery-National Historic Monument."

CHAPTER SIX

A humble feeling of respect, admiration, and wonder engulfs me whenever I enter a cemetery, especially one within the United States-and particularly those in Nevada. I find myself both mystified and matter-of-fact when within such hollowed grounds, especially since the U.S. government banned the use of such facilities in 2055. That change was made due to the over-saturation of such facilities. Congress enacted legislations barring the tradition of burials. If that process had been allowed to continue unabated, within several more centuries most land in the U.S., other than in national parks and various protected lands, would end up being used for either cemeteries or structures. Since the law was enacted, ElecticDustation has disposed of bodies. High-powered devices turn bodies into dust in seconds.

Cemeteries, especially those such as the one we were entering, seem other-worldly by modern standards. We progressed several hundred feet into the complex, until the point where the

Foot-Wheels track ended. After parking the unit into a public power source, we walked several blocks, passed hundreds of rows of graves, all laid flat-without those headstones that jut upward. It seems this facility had been among those that required headstones to be laid flat during the last several decades of its usual operation, to enable lawn-mowing devices to do their work without hindrance.

"Follow me, you sure walk slow," Annie observed, as we entered an adjoining cemetery, going under an archway that says: "Reno Masonic Cemetery: National Historic Site." Massive trees sprawled everywhere, on this flat area atop a hill that overlooks downtown Reno. Many rows are off-kilter slightly, apparently pushed to and froe through the decades by health tree roots, oblivious to the fact they should avoid the dead.

Momentarily, while standing side-by-side, almost as if we were distant relatives visiting a long-lost relative we have in common, Annie and I stood at a grave marked: "Virgil Bennett Ballard, April 27, 1927-April 27, 2025." I immediately was struck by the fact that not only did he die on his 98th birthday, but also his grave was lined with dozens of fresh flowers.

"Interesting," I observed.

"That's an understatement," Annie said, giving herself the sign of the cross, and kneeling beside the grave.

A fresh, clean scent filled the untainted high-mountain air, and I sensed this was a slight bit cooler than usual for this early in May. At ease and relaxed, but still wondering why this young woman had brought me there, I found myself looking at the grave, covered in bronze and still gleaming as if it had been installed just today. Then, I saw a poem, written across the middle of the headstone.

THE HIDDEN CHAMBER

> The mystery deepens–what could it be
> No one saw just what took place
> Time had sealed with rust and sand
> Weeds and debris hid the vaulted door

My first thought, upon reading this first verse, was how wondrous and majestic those words were, eerily appropriate for a graveyard such as this. I took a deep breath, and continued reading while Annie knelt, silently whispering a prayer. I can't say for sure why, maybe it was because those words were so moving, so touching, so plain, and so "real"–especially in a place such as this–that I began reading them aloud.

> But when opened the chamber inside
> Offered some clues to those who would explore
> Rumor spoke of a beauty, so overwhelming and rare
> No man could look upon her direct...

By this point, I began to realize that this poem, these very words surely must have been written by Virgil's much-more-famous brother. My heartbeat quickened, and I found myself speaking rapidly as I read.

> Else he would forever be turned to stone
> The chamber arranged mirrors held just so
> By reflection one could see her if she approved
> Those mirrors now lay shattered on the floor...

Holy heavens, who was he speaking of? My thoughts raced, as I wondered if perhaps Wes as a tribute wrote this poem to his beloved Bonnie Bowlander. Could it be that Virgil adored this poem so much, he chose to have it embossed on his own grave?

> The only writing that could be read
> Was chiseled in stone at the head of her bed
> But the whole chamber and stone had been split apart
> The letters—and V B were still intact
> Whatever their meaning, no one could guess
> As for the mystery of this broken chamber
> Could it have been a chamber in her heart?

Spellbound, and awestruck, I suddenly knelt beside the grave as well. What could this mean? Who was this love, this immortal beloved that had been etched in stone, spoken of so dearly? To me, it was as if written by a man-or someone-at least, who had a broken heart, of unrequited love, of passion unfulfilled, taken forward into the path of all eternity. A mystery had posed itself to me, and in that moment, at that very second, I knew that my passion would become to find an answer, for however long it took.

Then came a revelation, a new fact that left me even more stunned. Annie, it seems, had known what all this would do to me, how this setting would impact my very heart.

"This is my great-great-grandma's grave, or at least I think it is," Annie motioned to an adjoining headstone.

"That's your grandmother? That's Holly?"

"Well, at least I think it is. I found these graves just last week, and that's a primary reason why I decided to call you, and ..."

I stood and walked to the head of the adjoining grave. Right away, I realized that the headstone had no name. There were only these words: "Forbidden Fruit," and this headstone looked like that of Virgil Bennett Ballard's, except that the inscription was different.

"What could that mean, 'Forbidden Fruit?'" I yearned for as much detail as possible.

"I think I have an answer, and this is why I think it might be my great-grandmother in there," Annie said. "My mother had told me that it was my great-great-grandma, at least I think that's what she said, who had been given this poem by Virgil-for they had been deeply in love."

"You mean, Virgil gave this poem to Holly, and she's next to him, and . . ." As I mumbled, somewhat delighted to have this new mystery facing me-virtually the best and most magnetic of my career-Annie reached into her waist pocket, and pulled out a yellow piece of paper. She handed it to me, which I immediately read aloud.

FORBIDDEN FRUIT

Yes, I have tasted the forbidden fruit
And have sipped the heady wine
I now pursue a winding route
Much too difficult to define

I find myself totally hooked
That fruit tasted so divine
I keep remembering how it looked
To have it daily is my design

Gentle. Passionate. Eternal. A love, not fully satisfied. These words and phrases immediately raced through my mind, and I knew without question that within a very few minutes I would seek answers, as to who lay within this very grave. No mysterious love, especially one such as this, should ever go unresolved over so long a time.

"Well, what do you think?" Annie said matter-of-factly, as if we'd known each other always.

"You're asking me what I think, at a time like this? There's so much for me to absorb, you can't expect a detailed answer at this early point, can you?"

Annie stood beside me, and she began to brush her own hair. In that moment, she seemed so pretty, so gorgeous, so crisp in a good, young-adult way, looking like any woman would want to appear in youth. Here, in this graveyard, her youthful, bright aura seemed out of place-but somehow quite natural as well, for of course we all must die, we all must grow old-if we should be so lucky. No, Annie should have been ugly, and too-fat, and wrinkled, anything but a ravishing beauty in a place of death such as this.

"I'm going to find out who is in this grave for you, and then you'll have an answer."

"That's not what I'm asking, I think-I'm pretty sure it's my great-great grandmother. What I'm asking, is about details of the wreck."

"Stop!" I held out my hand, giving just that signal.

"What do you mean, stop?"

"Stop thinking this. Never assume something you think you know. If I've learned anything through the years, it's definitely that one should never assume a detail. You-we-need to find out who is in this grave."

From the sad, humble way Annie hung her head at that moment, looking down at her feet since the first time since I met her that morning, I sensed she believed I was right.

"Where is the office of this cemetery?" I asked her, sensing she might have an answer since she had been able to find Virgil's gave a few weeks ago.

"Oh, over there, it's a mason's museum-they keep the records."

"So, you've been there, and asked for the location of Virgil Ballard's grave? But you haven't asked who is buried beside him?"

"Well, yes, and no. Yes, I asked where his grave was, and no, I didn't ask about . . ." "Fine." I immediately started marching toward the office, with her following close behind. I was 51 years old, but at least at that point in my life, I was a strong, stout and vibrant man-not the frail, thin fellow that I've become today, just three years later.

Within five minutes, I had an answer. I knew who was in that grave marked "Forbidden Fruit." It was an answer that left this young woman stunned and increasingly perplexed.

And now that I had a name, I knew with certainty that it was time for intense research.

CHAPTER SEVEN

Annie remained speechless as we departed the cemetery complex. Before our visit there, I'm sure, she had herself convinced that her great-great-grandmother Holly, was in that grave beside that of Virgil B. Ballard.

And I'll have to admit, the response from that Masons official left me stunned as well. For the life of me, I've never heard of anyone reserving an empty grave, let alone put a headstone on one. At least, that's exactly what had happened in this case, at least according to that man, who wore a nameplate saying "Gary."

"We get asked that same question about every month or so, when curious people stumble upon it and come here into the office to ask," Gary said. "So don't feel embarrassed for asking that question. What I can tell you, there's an empty coffin in that grave, marked 'Forbidden Fruit.' It seems that, at least according to our records, several years before his death, Virgil Ballard had bought a plot next to one that had been designated for him. At the time, of course, those who operated this cemetery thought little of his request, which seemed normal to us at the time. According to legend, or at least word of mouth that's been passed down through the years, Virgil had told the cemetery staff that the plot would be used for the great love of his life, the woman he adored more than anyone. He refused to give her name to us, saying that when that person's time came-arrangements would be made. But in 2075, a half century after he passed in 2025, our cemetery staff-in honor of Mister Ballard-put an empty casket beside him, and they marked the empty grave the way he had wanted it to be, "Forbidden Fruit."

Speechless, Annie stood erect as if a statue beside Gary's desk as he gave these details. I sensed what Annie wanted to ask, but what she probably felt unable to-so I asked for her. "But what of Holly Johns?" I asked. "Have you ever heard of that person? Is there a record of a person by that name in this cemetery, or in the adjoining cemetery?"

Gary did a quick computer search, and gave a response that made my ears tingle: "That's funny, there isn't a single person named Holly buried in these two cemeteries-where at least 350,000 souls rest. Now, I wonder, what are the odds of that?"

"Respectfully, I'd have to say, it's not such odds I'm thinking about for the moment," I tried to be kind in saying this, while preparing to ask my next stupid question. "Who was Virgil Ballard? Where did he work? Did he have family around this area? And what about that poem on his headstone, 'The Hidden Chamber?' Where did that come from?"

Momentarily, Gary showed us an old tattered copy of a poem, written in a distinctive handwriting. Gary explained that this was the exact piece of paper Virgil Ballard had presented to personnel here, when he made arrangements for his own future funeral. "We kept this, as a courtesy to him, so that when the time came would be able to ensure that everything was done exactly as he requested." Gary set the book down on a table, so that we could inspect the poem further.

At that moment, Annie pulled the tattered old handwritten poem from her pocket. She put it beside the original from Virgil, and in an instant I realized the handwriting samples were an exact match. "We have something important here, a connection," I said, not bothering to relay the fact that I'm a certified expert in handwriting analysis. "Interesting? Who are you people?" Gary's energy level doubled.

"Just a state historical researcher. Nothing too important," I said, trying to downplay all this, but knowing full well I had stumbled upon perhaps the most intriguing historical case in Nevada history. "And what was it you know about Virgil Ballard's personal history?"

"I'm afraid that as a brother Mason of his, I'm unable to divulge those personal details-although I can, and of course have-spoken of his burial plot situation. Any discussion of those details has been authorized. As to his family, I can say that many of them are located here in this cemetery, and that he has many prominent descendants living in this community today. The other thing of note that I can say is that he was a prominent Realtor® here in town."

Satisfied that we had gotten about all the information we would be able to get, I escorted Annie from the building-while she remained mum. Once we arrived at her parked Foot-Wheels, she stayed silent as well, other than to tell me: "You drive."

Sensing she was undergoing a period of mental distress, I plopped into the device. She latched on behind me, latching her waist area to the metal hook on my back. I purposely avoided telling her that I hadn't driven one of these contraptions in maybe 30 years, and that I felt a bit uncomfortable doing so.

Nonetheless, right before heading away, I punched in the coordinates of our obvious destination. The Reno-Sparks Association of Realtors® Office would be an ideal stop to do some vital research, although I had just missed-unintentionally-its monthly luncheon.

CHAPTER EIGHT

"Is Monica Sloan here?" I asked a receptionist, the moment Annie and I entered the lobby of the association building, where it has been more than 110 years on Riggins Court off Meadow Wood Drive, near the former Meadowood Mall Shopping Complex, which is now a Sky Tube Hub Facility.

"Whom may I tell her is visiting?" the secretary seemed quite friendly but cordial, and I wished in that instant I had just such a person on my staff. Such cheery, bright and professional attitudes are hard to find these days. I guess some things never change.

Three minutes later, Monica greeted us, and invited us back to her sprawling office. Here, Monica impresses me at stoic, formal and methodical. That's a sharp contrast from when I see her on occasion coming or going from her home near mine, her overall demeanor in those situations always seeming cheery and free-flowing. This time, after exchanging the usual, obligatory

61

pleasantries such as comments on the weather and whatnot, I apologized to her for missing this afternoon's lunch, and promised I'd try again in June if she'd still allow me to. She said no apologies were necessary, and that I'm always welcome.

"Why we're here, what I'd like to ask you-do you have any information in here on Virgil Ballard, who was a Realtor® based in Reno in the late 1900s and early this century?"

"Do I?" Monica sat erect, grinning broadly. "Of course, I do-in fact, you're sitting near a picture of him."

As Annie did the same beside me, I turned to the right, and sure enough, there was a huge photograph, of a man. The colorful picture was blown up, larger than life size. There was Virgil Ballard, for my own satisfied eyes to behold. He stood in front of a horse barn, arm-in-arm with a woman in her senior years-about his age as well. Under the photo, a plaque was embossed in large, bold letters: "Virgil and Ruth." Underneath this was a brief written description of his many accomplishments in the realty industry.

"May I ask, who is that woman with him? And why do you have his picture here?"

Monica stood up at her desk, and for the first time-I'm surprised I never recognized this before-I noticed that she's statuesque. Her bosom full and fine, her posture immaculate, her shoulders perched back at an exquisite angle. It was as if Monica was a trained runway model, almost as if a contestant in a beauty pageant who happened to wear snappy, sharp business clothes, as she walked up to the photos. "Virgil was then, and he remains today, one of the most respected Realtors® in northern Nevada, and in much of the West as well," Monica said, her posture suddenly a bit more relaxed than it had been before. Right away, I remembered that Monica's husband is a professional weight trainer and body builder. Boy, must he have fun at home. "Virgil was an important pioneer in our industry, and his business philosophies remain paramount among all local real estate industry workers in our area to this day. The company he personally founded, Ballard Co., Inc., continues to thrive to this day, well over a century after it was founded, and it's main office is still over on Brinkby Avenue, near the former Peppermill Hotel-Casino, which of course now is the Spring-Regency Resort & Spa."

"That woman," Annie finally piped up, as she stood at the couch she had just been sitting on beside me. Tears welled in Annie's eyes, as her cheeks turned redder than Washington apples. "That's Ruth? It says Ruth Laurene Cracraft Saunders?"

"Yes?" Monica seemed puzzled.

"She ... She ... She's ... She was ..."

"I know, tell her," I couldn't help but interrupt.

"She was my great-great-great-grandmother!" Annie almost screamed this. "She's beautiful! Look at her! Look at that woman! She's beautiful! I came from her! I'm from her, and ..."

"What in the world is this all about?" Monica's expression quickly turned from pride to puzzlement. Instead of a beauty pageant contestant, this time she looked as if an upset mother whose child had just spilled milk-although she also somehow seemed compassionate.

"So, it wasn't Holly! It was Ruth! I didn't even know Ruth existed!" Annie spoke non-stop, as if her mind had been a dam that broke-after holding back oceans filled with intense emotion, deep from within her heart. Everything poured forth, and suddenly I started learning the truth about this young woman's thoughts, and dreams. "Ruth! Ruth! She's the one I've been hearing so much about, that my family has spoken of through all these years! I was wrong. It wasn't Holly. It was Ruth. She's the one who was in love with Virgil Ballard-and he loved her madly, truly, with all his heart as well."

Mystified, Monica suddenly sat down in the seat where Annie had been just a minute earlier. As if an attentive high school student, itching to impress her teacher, Monica sat erect-attentively focused on Annie's every word. It was almost as if Monica had become a dutiful marionette, as though she was taught and stretched by strings from the ceiling-tied to her willing back.

"Thank you! Thank you! Thank you, Mister Rivera!" Annie pranced over to me, and gave me a giant, wet, loving peck clean across my willing forehead. "You've proven it, and I know it's true. It was Virgil Ballard that wrote that famous poem-not his brother!"

"What!" This revelation stunned me. "What are you trying to say?"

"Aren't you hearing me, Mister Rivera? It was Virgil that wrote that famous poem, 'Looking Back,' and not his poor brother, Wes-who was killed in that wreck!"

"I'm, what . . ."

"Can't you see, it's obvious? My ancestor, someone in my family tree was the inspiration for that poem, and those many other poems that have enraptured the world!"

A long silence followed. Annie gave an emphatic, encouraging expression, as if she expected me to express instant agreement. And for her part, Monica now displayed an expression of both surprise and bewilderment-as if one of the biggest, most important revelations in world history had just been made right there in her esteemed office.

"Now, Annie," I stood, reaching for the young woman's arms, gently, as if a father trying to comfort and calm his overly excited daughter. I genuinely empathized with what she was going through. "Nothing has been proven in that regard. Nothing. Something like that, the authenticity of who wrote an important poem, needs much more scholarly research and verification. There must be a period of research, and . . ."

"Then, you're a fake, if you can't accept it," Annie pulled her hand, sharply, in a flash, from mine. "I was afraid you'd do this. You're hiding behind haughty, highbrow, snooty intellectualism. Why do you need to do research, to recognize the obvious?"

Right there in the presence of my next-door neighbor, I-one of the most revered state public officials, or at least so I assumed-started to bicker openly with a person I had only met face-to-face that very morning. Our shouting became so heated and intense, that I'm sure all workers could hear us in the entire building. Yet through it all, Monica stayed put in her seat, making not a move to interrupt.

At the height of our bickering, I sensed that if Annie were ever to find solitude and happiness that she so desperately seemed to yearn for, she must learn to relax, and to accept the world-for whatever is, simply "is."

CHAPTER NINE

As calm and relaxed as possible considering the situation, I sat back in a lounge chair in my back yard. It had been two weeks since I met Annie and visited the cemetery, a period of local, national and international controversy resulting from that one day. For the first time since then, I finally had this chance to get a bit of much-needed daytime rest. As Carolina lay down inside our nearby home for an afternoon nap, I turned off a Cyber-Radio next to me, sipped a cool ice tea, and listened to birds chirp. For the life of me, I couldn't remember how long it had been since I had taken such time for reflection.

I've always enjoyed late spring afternoons before the weather gets miserably hot. This was just such a moment, when lawn irrigators made that faint whirring sound. I closed my eyes, took a long, deep, slow breath, and allowed my thoughts to slow down to a nice steady pace. In that second, it felt almost as if I had taken a sedative, some sort of magic pill that made all that spinning from my head go away.

I started going through my CyberMails, and came upon a notice that my 30-year high school reunion would be held July 25-28 at the Fairmont Hotel in San Francisco. My first inclination upon seeing this was to avoid the event, since I obviously would be home at that time caring for my wife as her cancer-filled body slowly wasted away. Still, seeing this invitation made me think of my old girlfriend, Patty Carnahan. Through the years, despite my closeness with Carolina, I've often wondered what became of Patty. Did she stop communicating with me back then, because she had fallen in love with some other fellow in Hawaii? Did Patty ever think of me, the way I did her? At times, only to myself, I had to admit I never fell out of love with her-not just the dream of her, but who she was, what was in her soul, and how we melded together in our youthful passions. At the moment, there in my peaceful back yard, I made a pledge that someday soon, after my personal life settled down, I would do a little research to discover whatever happened to Patty. Surely, I never would look her up directly, for doing that-from my mind-would have been inappropriate after all these many years. Using my C-Pad, I started a note to myself to do that background check.

And, then, wouldn't you know, as often is the case when such pleasant moments occur, my earphone rang. Since so much had been going on, I decided to answer, in case another emergency had erupted.

"Hello, Mister Rivera?" "Yes, Annie, hello."

"I hope you don't mind. I have my monitor turned on, so you can see me. I thought it would be important for you to see my reactions, so you can sense my emotions—where I'm coming from on the way things have turned out."

Sure enough, I saw a clear, distinct image of Annie on right side of my eyeglasses. Ah, the miracles of technology. For all I knew, she was 500 miles away in Las Vegas at the moment. But at least I could see her.

"Yep. Clear image."

"I would like to apologize to you."

"For what, Annie? None is necessary."

"How was I to know that lady from the real estate association was going to issue a press release that very afternoon-telling the entire world that your office was investigating a claim that that famous poem wasn't really written by Wes Ballard."

"Well, young lady, you got the notoriety you wanted. I saw you this morning on the cover of USA Today, and you didn't look half bad the other day on 'Good Morning World.'"

"I don't care about the publicity. I honesty care about the fact your office, and the governor's administration has received much embarrassment. It's as if you were caught with your shorts down, the way the news media is behaving-just because you don't, or didn't, know whatever became of my great-great-grandmother, Ruth."

"Don't worry. I have every reason to believe that we'll have some pretty good answers in a day or two. And as to your claim that Virgil wrote the poem, that's an entirely different matter and even with today's technology, it'll take some time to . . ."

"Stop. Mister Rivera, I know all that. Please stop playing me for a fool. I've seen all those quotes from you, in that regard in the media. How stupid do you think I am, sir? I'm just calling you, because I'm concerned. I just heard a news report that the governor is considering whether to fire you, and the press even asked him about it at this morning's news conference."

"Young woman, I'm a big boy, believe me, and I can handle it," I tried to take a soft, even tone-hoping to hide the fact that although I hate my job with a dread, I never would want it to end that way. Right away, I saw Carolina standing at the sliding back door of our home, looking gaunt, but giving me a weak smile as if to show she loved me. "Annie, a more important issue is whether you've decided to sell that voice recording of JJ Ballard-for I know it's worth a fortune, and the Mormon Church would want it, not to mention quite a few museums. My office has verified its authenticity."

"How."

"I don't have the time at the moment to give you details," I smiled at Carolina, as she approached me. "Annie, something has come up. I must leave now." "Can I call you again? Will you let me know what you find out about Ruth, what became of her-and any details you can dig up on her relationship with Virgil."

"You have my word, I will. Bye now." I took Carolina's hand, as she sat down in a lawn chair next to mine.

Dark circles larger than caves surrounded Carolina's eyes, which once had been so blue and lively they made me excited just to think of them. Now, though, they reflected nothing but death-coming death, certain death, unavoidable death.

"Ben, I love you so. My only regret is that we haven't been able to spend more time together. You know how much I ..."

Poor Carolina's head drooped forward as her eyes closed. Her head slumped back, and her mouth moved wide open. I had not expected this so soon, this death, this change, this sudden robbery of my domestic tranquility. I gasped loudly then, hit by the reality that in that instant, without time to say goodbye, without even a whisper, I didn't even get a chance to say goodbye. No heroic measures to save her life in that moment, for she hadn't wanted to live as a vegetable. No shaking her, for she looked so peaceful. No sounds. No voices. Just my tears, falling one after another, repetitively, onto the concrete of our back patio-and that's all there was, in that moment, of the world as once again Mother Nature robbed me of potential happiness.

CHAPTER TEN

"**B**oss, I didn't expect you back into the office so soon." Even Ruby, at that very moment, from the doorway of my office, was showing empathy and concern for me-for once. "I'm so, so sorry for your loss. Words can't...."

"I didn't expect the end to come for her so soon," I found myself rattling personal details, the kind of information I usually guard from my office staff-especially Ruby. "I had planned to take the last several weeks off, to spend every moment with her. I feel..."

"It's okay, sir." "So guilty, and..."

Beverly, my secretary popped into the doorway beside Ruby, and interrupted: "Boss, sorry to break this up, but it's the governor on the line for you. Sounds important."

"Sure, I'll take it," I flicked my earphone, as Ruby and Beverly scooted out the door, back into the main staff area. "Yes, governor. I'm glad that you called."

"Ben, the First Lady and I want you to know our hearts and our prayers are with you at this time," he sounded genuinely concerned, but as always with this guy-at least from my perspective-there always was a sense that perhaps he was up to no good. "I encourage you now, to take all the time off from work that you need. I called now, partly because I'm so surprised to learn that you're back in your office so soon."

"Governor, you have my word that I'll find out every detail possible about the Ballard history, and get down to the facts of the matter. I came in to work, because I know how important the Ballard case is to you-and I realize how much pressure you've been under-in media scrutiny because of this case."

"Ben, you know, I genuinely appreciate that. Now that you mention it, the media has been making this whole thing into a huge story. For the life of me, I swear, I never realized how that blasted poem-and the resulting song, and the movie, and all the books-are so overwhelming popular worldwide, until all this fuss kicked up like a dust-devil blowing across the desert."

"Sir, some media stories have a life of their own."

"Did your staff find out anything much of any substance yet, on this Ruth woman? Maybe you could put a crunch on details, make up something, squish this whole thing, and make it go away..."

"The press loves a good fight, a controversy, especially when it involves a romance-particularly one from what these days we call the Old West-and by today's standards, the 1930s, and '40s, and even the '50s-fit the bill, although those decades fell more than a half century after the actual 'cowboy era' came to a close. From the way reporters are treating this story, it's as if they've found out that Teddy Roosevelt really was a transvestite or that even John Fitzgerald Kennedy was a 'closet Republican.'"

Hearing this, the governor broke out in that trademark genuine, gut-powered laughter that he's so famous for. He wallowed and guffawed so much on the other side of the phone I could almost picture his huge belly bouncing up and down like a bowl of gelatin.

"You're great, Ben, no matter what some people say about you. I hope you take that the right way. All I ask is that you keep me informed on any major developments. I don't want to get caught by any surprises, the media asking me questions that I should know answers to . . . You get the idea?" "Governor, this is a case that demands answers, that needs meticulous research. The faster I can get you the accurate details-and find out what happened-whatever the case may be, the sooner we'll be able to put this case to rest, and move on to other matters."

"Nothing could make me happier. Hell, this case has drawn so much international curiosity that my office staff has been getting calls on this from Japan, and Australia, and Central China-you name it. People everywhere love the romance. They love the intrigue. Maybe we could use this to the state's advantage. You know, tourism?"

"Whatever you say, governor. I'll give it some thought. Meanwhile, believe me, we'll get down to the truth."

"Goodbye, Ben. Talk to you soon."

I gently hung up, thinking of how much I hated this bastard politician, who looked like that famous egg Humpty Dumpty, at least as far as I was concerned. The nerve of that guy, Governor Clarence Codelcous, irked me. Even the mere sound of his name made me cringe. For him to suggest screwing up the details on this historical research, just to bring more visitors into Nevada, made my blood boil. Right then and there, I knew I'd be far happier if only we had a seasoned, mature governor-instead of this glad-handing backslapper.

Momentarily, Ruby poked her head back into the doorway: "We just got some mighty interesting developments, into our research on Ruth. This new information is good enough to make your socks curl right off your feet, and your hair stick straight up from the top of your head. Can I come into your office, sir?"

"By all means, Ruby. Nothing would make me happier-and goodness knows, a little good news might cheer me up. I've been trying to get a lift for days." "What I have to report to you is all about Ruth! Sir, we've hit a major jackpot, and found some vital information on her-even when we weren't looking for it . . ."

CHAPTER ELEVEN

Many of history's most ingenious discoveries came quite by accident, or at least when they weren't expected amid research. Consider when Alexander Fleming discovered penicillin in his famous "mould in a Petri dish experiment," a finding that eventually saved millions of people who otherwise would have died or lost their limbs from bacterial infections.

Just as amazing, when Alexander Graham Bell uttered on March 10, 1876, "Watson, come here. I want you," that famous inventor accidentally discovered he was capable of transmitting voice over electromagnetic lines. The most famous accidental discovery of all, of course, came on July 27, 2017, when Jessica Covington used a Isomagnetics Rod to project sunlight onto a piece of paper, burning it-and discovering technology that later was used to develop today's clean and abundant non-fossilized, and non-nuclear energy.

From my way of thinking, my office staff's discovery of an old tape recording of Ruth Laurene Cracraft Saunders is just as pivotal to world history-especially among those people who cherish and covet fine literature. This discovery was so accidental, so unexpectedly, that the voice recording itself was almost overlooked-not even reviewed by my staff when it was initially found. Ruby explained the basic background details as soon as she sat down in a chair across from my desk, beside one of our other cracker-jack researchers, South Africa native Motamubi Kamuba.

Ruby revealed that our staff had received the recording a week before Annie even phoned me, and it came from a much different source.

At that pivotal meeting in my office, Ruby held up the recording to show what it looked like, an odd looking piece of plastic with two holes in it.

"This came from inside the cornerstone of a 96-year-old building in Reno."

"A cornerstone?" I was instantly perplexed at how such an amazing, historically significant discovery could have come from such an obvious place. "That's right, sir, a cornerstone," Motamubi said, a huge smile across his face. "It was from the Rollan Melton Elementary School on Robb Drive in Reno. The building was demolished for a reconstruction project, on the morning of last April 17. And, in keeping with traditions, of course, the cornerstone's contents were sent by the school's reconstruction company to our office for evaluation."

The basic process of reviewing items that had been stored in cornerstones had become old-hat to me through the years. In fact, I'd estimate my office receives at least four separate crates of cornerstone contents daily, as increasing numbers of old public buildings and major business structures, and even churches, statewide are razed for reconstruction or refurbishing projects. Mostly beginning in the 1700s, in a nationwide tradition that continued well into the early part of this century, construction crews or people that financed building projects had a habit of putting memorabilia into cornerstones. Such items depended on whims and fancies of those involved. Most of these cornerstone installations, some lacking any ceremony whatsoever-where others entailed lavish ceremonies-usually entailed encasing newspapers from those days, along with items from the buildings fanciers or planners-such as architectural maps and the like.

Anyway, with the amount of extensive detail we now have on those early days, as the 22nd century approaches some folks might think these items would be considered mundane or worthless. Yet for the most part, except where obvious junk is involved, nothing could be further from the truth. My office staff frequently gets high Dollar-Max offers on such items, which remain so rare and difficult to find many people will do just about anything they can to obtain such items-which soar in value due to their extreme rarity. This seems natural, for, after all, most 1900s-eara items of good quality were either lost, thrown away, or destroyed during the horrific wars of early this century, especially World War III-when entire societies parted with anything they could in order to survive.

"Is this recording of Ruth?" I asked, puzzled.

"Yes, we're 100-percent positive it is?" Motamubi said. "You doubt this, boss?"

"We'll play it for you right now boss!" Ruby proclaimed. "We've only listened to the first few minutes of it ourselves, and ..."

"No! You will not play that recording now! Not a single word, not an iota of this tape will be heard by anyone until one important thing happens?"

"What's that, sir? What are you waiting for?"

"Can't you understand the obvious?" I grew immediately frustrated, and I suppose this is about the period when just about every question started to strike me as "stupid." I hadn't ever felt that way before then, at least as far as I could recall. "Well, we all seem ready to hear it in its entirety. I see no reason for delay." Motamubi seemed uncharacteristically impatient; he obviously was proud of his major discovery and wanted it studied and reviewed as soon as possible.

I stood at my desk, and tried to remain calm: "Hold on here, wait. Don't dare play that recording, and I don't care how valuable it is, or how rare it is, or how important it might seem-we're going to wait until Annie May Johns can be summoned here. Annie is the closest living ancestor of Ruth, at least the one ancestor of hers that we work with, and I've promised the young woman she would get every major detail-every SIGNIFICANT detail-right along with us as it's first revealed. And this, my friends, is just such a moment."

Ruby stood, and faced me from the opposite side of my desk: "But sir, that woman-Annie May Johns-has been a royal pain in the ass. Did you know that? Did you know she calls me, or other co-staffers here, at least three times a day to nag us for details-for facts on any new developments in this case? She's more persistent than Zorba the Greek, and more vicious than Alexander the Conqueror as far as I'm concerned. Holy cow, she's even peskier than the news media, and that's saying a lot."

Still holding the plastic device, Motamubi stood as well: "Ben, I'll have to agree with Ruby on this one. We have no idea what all the details are that will come out in this tape. If any unexpected revelations occur, word could leak if . . ." "People, sit down, now," I motioned for them to do that. "I respect your opinions, but I've given my word to this young woman-and I never break my word."

I then flicked the intercom, to make a request of my secretary, Beverly: "Please summon Annie May Johns to this office. I want her here within 10 minutes. A very important revelation is about to be made here, that she will want to participate in"

"Sir, I'd imagine she's in Las Vegas, working at the Luxor, and she wouldn't be able to travel here until after she gets off, and . . ."

"You still think she works at the Luxor?" I showed my obvious amazement, since I thought just about everyone had heard the news. "Miss Johns is a billionaire now-already-because she sold the tape recording of cowboy and rancher JJ Ballard to the Mormon Church for a fortune. It seems the whole world wanted to own that tape . . ."

"Forgive me," Beverly's voice echoed over the intercom, showing obvious respect for me-especially since it was rare of her to fail to notice such important detail. "Then, where can I get a hold of her?"

"Try the Hilton Hotel in Tampa, Florida," I said. "She told me she would be on vacation there, and that she would get here in a flash if anything happened. Just call her regular Ear-Phone number anyway. I'm sure the satellites will find her."

"Sure, give me a second." Beverly said always efficient and to the point. While awaiting her answer, I sat down and sat across from Ruby and Motamubi. As beads of perspiration began to glisten on their foreheads, I didn't want to tell the pair that I was just as anxious to hear that recording as they.

Then, unexpectedly, I began to cough at my desk, hacking so loudly, and with such persistence that Ruby stood up out of concern. My coughing continued, and I realized I had phlegm coughing up from my lungs.

This pneumonia had been slashing through my body the past several days, and I'd been trying to hide it. Even the nastiest Bio-Cuticles, guaranteed effective on 99.9 percent of all patients, had failed to put a dent in it. I'd lost seven pounds in the previous three days.

"Boss, you should go home," Ruby went around the desk and cradled my arm, as I grabbed for some tissue from my desk. "Everyone here has seen how overworked and ill you've been, but you refuse to admit it." "Stop sounding like a wife, my own wife never nagged me as much as you, and . . ."

"Sir, good news," Beverly came back onto the intercom line. "I caught up with Annie in Palm Springs, California, and she said she'll be here in about ten minutes."

"Fine. Thank . . . Thank . . . Thank you," I couldn't hold back, and started coughing more. I hated being seen this way, in such a weak position, especially by those people such as Ruby and Motamubi, who had an edgy relationship with me. "I'm okay. I said, 'I'm okay!' Now, you two sit back down please."

"But sir, you're health, and . . ." Ruby tried to start one of those long lectures she has grown famous for during the few previous years. At least some folks appreciated this feisty gal for her up-front, no-holds-barred attitude, which I consider rather odd considering the fact she once studied to become a nun-but later changed her mind about pursuing that career, for a reason she never has revealed.

"I am not the reason we're here in this room," I paused momentarily, to cough into the tissue. "Before Annie gets here, I think we can review some basics that are necessary for each of us to know-the kinds of details I can fill the young woman in on later."

I then asked why in the world the tape was put into the elementary school's cornerstone. Motamubi gave a measured, logical response, leaving no doubt that his theory must have been correct. Once again, he held up the plastic-covered tape, and this time I noticed that these words clearly had been written on it: "Rollan Melton oral history interview, April 10, 2000." But in listening to the first several minutes of the tape, before turning it off and coming to my office, Motamubi and Ruby had discovered that the voice clearly, undoubtedly was that of Ruth Laurene Cracraft Saunders.

I was told the interview with Ruth, was conducted by Wayne Melton, the noted biographer, novelist, actor and screenwriter. But Wayne Melton's other numerous works had included extensive taped interviews with his father, Rollan Melton, the newspaper's columnist and the elementary school's namesake.

Since there were no other recordings in the cornerstone, other than the one "Virgil Ballard interview," which Motamubi and Ruby hadn't heard yet, the possible reason seemed obvious. Wayne Melton, known as meticulous researcher and prolific writer and actor, must have goofed-sending the tapes of his interviews with Ruth and Virgil to the school's administrators for the cornerstone ceremony-rather then the interviews with his father. Thus, if, in this research my office staff is able to conclude without a reasonable doubt that this scenario is what happened, the biography books on Wayne Melton will have to be reopened and rewritten.

At that moment, without telling my associates aloud, I had to admit to myself that this case-the research into Ruth and Virgil-had evolved into the most complex, compelling and interesting of my career. And, to this day, more than three years after that fateful morning when Ruby and Motamubi brought those materials in my office, I have yet to hear of a single state archivist in any other state having a case this juicy, enticing, and even romantic. Of course, at that point I realized more specifics of the meaningful and true love between Virgil and Ruth must be brought into the surface. And certainly there remained the question of whether Virgil had written that famous poem "Looking Back," and not his famous brother. While the love story interested me most during this phase, with each passing moment I found myself facing the fact that the authenticity and origin of the poem might matter most to the world.

"Hello, you sent for me?" Annie poked her head into my doorway. This time, she had a cheery, bright smile. "I got here as fast as I could." "Ten minutes to get here?" I wanted to joke, to lighten the mood. I realized everyone present was tense, excited and eager to discover more. "My goodness, it took you this long to get all the way up here from Palm Springs?"

"What's going on?" Annie hustled into the room. Gone was the poor but gorgeous waif I had just met a few months before. By this point, Annie had transformed herself into a dazzling, cover girl-style ball of energy. Her sparkling, long, curly hair proved a sharp contrast to her drab, dull, hanging mane from just a few weeks earlier. And, now, she wore a sky-blue, sequined gown, the neckline so dangerously low that I found myself thinking about sex-only momentarily, mind you-for the first time since poor Carolina's death. "My boyfriend is out in the lobby. Can he come in her, too?"

"Boyfriend? You didn't tell me you had a boyfriend." I observed, as Ruby and Motamubi smiled broadly, greeting Annie as if they loved her-when, of course, I knew quite the opposite was the case. "I hope you don't mind, but due to the sensitivity of what we're about the discover, I think it would be best if he stayed outside."

Annie avoided issuing any complaints in this regard, although I thought I heard her mumble to herself—"bureaucrat"—but I let it go, because at least she wasn't asking any stupid questions. Annie seemed to sense that we would tell of any important details we could. We quickly gave her the basic rundown. "Start the recording, please," I asked Motamubi. He flicked a few buttons, but nothing happened. But still, there was no success, not even the noise of a pin drop. "Sorry. Sorry, sir. We had it working just a while ago. Please understand that the power sources back then were antiquated, and they don't easily adapt to anything we have today."

Sure enough, in the last three quarters of the 1900s, and into the first several decades of this century, people plugged wires into the their home and office walls in order to connect their electrical devices into power grids. Since such devices became antiquated long ago, Motamubi has had to jerry rig some SunSorcers code holders at the two forked-shaped wires that in the old days went into antiquated, cumbersome contraptions called "electrical outlets." Angry with himself for failing to solve this dilemma, Motamubi began twisting and adjusting a variety of knobs and buttons. Frustrated, he finally said, "I just can't seem to get it going." At just that moment, the tape started whirling, turning round-and in that instant we started hearing words from that woman nearly 100 years ago. The interviewer started off by announcing that it was Jan. 10, 2002, and that he was about to interview Ruth Laurene Saunders of Sandy, Utah.

Needless to say, upon hearing this, Annie began to beam as if a virgin bride at her wedding. To me, her smile seemed full, innocent, and full of wonder, a perfect match to her rosy cheeks-which seemed a sharp contrast to her dazzling gown. Ruth started off by saying that except for occurrences of the past several years prior to the recording date, the best, most glorious developments in her life were having her daughters. On that day, they ranged in age from 42 to 54; Laura Louise, born Nov. 15, 1948; Kathleen Ruth, born July 18, 1950; Marsha Lynn, March 3, 1954; Stacie Rae, Nov. 25, 1958; and Holly Ann, Dec. 13, 1960. The worst tragedies had been the death of her own sister, Betty Aloha, who died of kidney disease; and the tragic death by gunshot wound of one of her beloved grandsons.

Five minutes after the interview began, Melton asked Ruth "how you would want to be remembered 100 years from now." Without missing a beat, Ruth said, "I think I would want them to remember me as being fair, loving, and a good mother, and a good friend. I guess if people remember me for that, I would be happy..." Yet in a subsequent revelation, Ruth admitted essentially to being "human." Those weren't her precise words here, just my own conclusion based on how she described herself, her choices of words honest and forthright. "I am stubborn, feisty, and often want my own way. That's just the way I turned out."

With those basics taken care of, Melton started getting the chronology of Ruth's life. She remembered feeling lonely between ages 5 and 10, primarily because she desperately missed her "real" father, for her parents had been divorced when she was 3 or 4. "And I would always think about him. And although my step-dad was kind and loving, I'd think I missed something that my real dad and I had. I never admitted this to my mother."

At this point in the interview, I noticed Ruby and Motamubi sit on the edges of their chairs, and it became obvious to me that they hadn't heard the recording past this point. Annie's face became expressionless, which seemed out of place with her clothing and her shapely body, which spoke volumes. It was almost as if she was hypnotized, mesmerized by the riveting words of her great-great-great grandmother.

"Even to this day, I can remember when I was about 3, and my real dad was working on a windmill, and I can remember him saying to my momma, 'Laura, bring a hammer.' And I somehow got the hammer and I started climbing this windmill. So there I was high up on this windmill for all the world to see, and my dad was at the top of the windmill, looking down at me-how I must have seemed to him, a little girl conquering the universe, I suppose. And my mother finally came out in the yard, and she saw me perched like a robin way up there, and she started to yell: 'Ruth, come down here!' And that's when, finally, I could tell they were scared, but I wasn't scared. Frantic, my dad climbed down and he got me. . . ." Enraptured by Ruth's soothing, mellow and highly feminine voice, I could sense that the four of us in the room would remember this moment for the rest of our lives-for this story already was riveting, certainly a tale that biographers would chronicle and analyze in many different ways for decades, or perhaps even centuries to come. I sensed that the three of us yearned for Ruth to rush through her story, and get to the part where she meets Virgil. Yet perhaps failing at the time to realize the historical significance of her relationship with him, and of how the mystery of their love would one day capture the imagination of the world, she dutifully answered Melton's questions.

Partly because she was only a child, little Ruth didn't know her biological father's profession. By the time she was 5 years old, her mother moved with her new husband and Ruth's siblings from

Englewood, California, in a burgeoning urban area, to the desolate, small high desert town of Winnemucca, Nevada. Their family had followed Ruth's grandmother, who owned and operated boarding houses. It was this grandmother, Estella, who had helped Ruth's stepfather find work there as an auto mechanic.

Shortly after moving to Winnemucca, the entire family became enraptured at an unexpected discovery, that Ruth-at an early age-possessed artistic talents. From early childhood, she started making lavish, colorful hats, winning widespread compliments among adults throughout town.

Upon hearing this, Annie briefly touched her own hat, a small, light dainty number accented by a colorful feather-which I considered appropriate for summer in Palm Springs, but not for a state government office in Nevada of all places.

Ruth confessed that while her mother, Laura Marguerite had been kind, loyal and loving-dutifully accepting and completing any task her husband demanded-Ruth was much different from an early age, for "I was always head-strong, with a mind of my own." Laura loved her own mother, Grandma Estella, who was rather domineering, a characteristic that little Ruth possessed.

Poor but far from starving, little Ruth lived with her family in a dilapidated old home, where there were no bathrooms-only an outhouse. Every Saturday all the kids would take turns having their baths in a tub in the middle of the kitchen. Besides Ruth's biological sister, Betty, the child who would later die as a young adult of liver disease, the others were a stepsister-also named Betty-and a step-brother, Robert, plus half brothers Dick, Jim, and Owen. Like almost all American families during the later years of the Great Depression in the late 1930s, and during the advent of

World War II in the early 1940s, the family lived mostly on what little their breadwinners could earn.

By the time Ruth was 10 she had mousy brown hair, and she didn't consider herself very cute-a sharp contrast from her mother, who although petite was curvaceous and gorgeous, a ravishing beauty. Hearing this, I started once again to look at Annie across the table from me, her enticing countenance and body much fuller than those described by her ancestor.

Ruth's biggest embarrassment came at age 11 when a kind and concerned elementary school teacher sent her home from school early to give Ruth's mother a note. It had just one sentence: "Buy Ruth a bra." Although still a pre-teen, Ruth's bosom had suddenly grown full and erect, much earlier than other girls her age-and her own family had either overlooked this development, or they had been too shy or poor to give this child the proper support she so desperately needed.

"The lady-that teacher, Dixie Weickle-she was just trying to keep me from being embarrassed," Ruth said. "And I was embarrassed about that, because my young boobs jiggled, and they got me lots of attention-especially from the boys. This made me feel uncomfortable, since I was shy by nature."

It was during the fourth or fifth grade when Ruth's best friend became Virgil Bennett Ballard's little sister, Joaquina, several years his junior. But because of her tender age, Ruth never paid attention to him-or at least she hardly knew he existed.

During summers and winters in the high desert, Ruth and her sister-often accompanied by Joaquina-would walk nearly three miles one-way to school. Harsh weather conditions sometimes proved bothersome, especially during extremely cold winters when their families worked hard to keep adequate supplies of galoshes and sturdy shoes.

"I remember it getting so cold that one day while we were walking to school, a boy named Brett Culverhouse made the mistake of putting his tongue on the railroad tracks," Ruth said. "That was one of the worst things Brett could have done, because his tongue was literally frozen to the metal, and he couldn't move. And when a train was coming, desperate to save himself, Brett literally had to-with all his might-pull himself from the tracks, leaving a portion of his ripped-out tongue on the rail. This sounds like I'm making it up, but it's true-every word."

This revelation riveted the four of us who were listening to the recording, largely I suppose because railroads are now hailed as more romantic than ever. They've long since become a thing of the past. From the perspective of those of us in the late 21st century, this is doubly fascinating, since Winnemucca has become a no-man's zone due to nuclear radiation fallout. Thus, to hear the actual words and descriptions of someone who lived in that area makes everything come to life, at least in the mind.

"It got so cold, I can remember my full sister Betty and I putting our hands under cold water at school-to make them feel warm," Ruth said. "Of course, we hated it at the time, because the cold felt like death itself-but remembering it literally makes me all warm inside, feeling alive and fresh, mostly because that was about the time I met Virgil, that I started paying attention to him."

Still, Ruth remembers herself as being far from beautiful, a sharp contrast to her older step-sister, Betty Louise, who had much fuller, more "womanly" bosom-and a face that made everyone who saw her think she was super-attractive. Normally, this difference failed to bother Ruth. But one day her attitude all changed, at least for a brief time. This transition happened shortly after Ruth bought herself a special, enticing Easter jacket-using her own money, which she had earned at a menial hospital job at age 14. "But Betty Louise got it before I did. She simply got up the nerve, opened the box, and wore it right to school for everyone to see-and nobody thought anything of it, as if it were her own."

Now, as State Archivist, in my own summary and observations at hearing this section of the recording, I began to surmise that although Ruth described herself as feisty-she actually had a kind, loving heart-so much so, that perhaps at least in those early years people "walked" all over her, at least to a degree. It seemed almost as if she yearned to be taken care of, to be coveted and cherished, which can only happen in the way that a strong, masculine but sensitive guy can provide a woman.

Betty Louise had pulled off the Easter dress-stealing caper although she was two years older than Ruth. In fact, Betty Louise was so stingy, she could have bought a similar dress for herself but refused. Instead, she chose to mooch off her younger, more naive step-sister. To be sure, as Ruth's interview revealed, Betty Louise saved every penny she earned working as a teller in Humboldt County Bank, the same financial institution the notorious bandits Butch Cassidy and the Sundance Kid had robbed 40 years earlier as the true horse-and-buggy days as the old West waned to a close.

Still, even during the years that Ruth grew up there, Winnemucca remained a town founded and that continually depended upon good old American roots-railroad work, mining jobs and even agriculture and cattle despite the high desert terrain. Despite their rough life during a difficult economy for everyone, Ruth's parents managed to get along famously with each other. Ruth's stepfather worshipped her mother, enraptured by her sweetness, capped off by that flowing dark hair that once went as long as her waist, and that petite but super-feminine figure that helped make him the envy of every man in town.

Hearing Ruth give this vivid description made Annie beam in obvious pride. Even Ruby, not necessarily known as being happy or laughable in any respect, started smiling broadly. All along, as the recording continued, Motamubi's expression remained dour and worrisome, making me worry that perhaps he sensed something was getting technically wrong with the recording system.

Be that as it may, Ruth explained that her grandmother, Estella, had hailed from Rathburn, Idaho. There, she had married a man whose own father had been born on a boat while en route from Great Britain to America. But during that same excursion, the infant's parents died from a sudden illness that also killed hundreds of other passengers on the same excursion. Concerned, and out of what they felt was their Christian duty, a family on the same excursion summarily adopted the infant on the spot and moved with him to Idaho. Forever hailed as Stacy Nelson by his new family, the lad started studying at an early age to be a preacher. Stacy grew up to be highly cooperative, following the wishes of just about everyone he met. This later proved to be a sharp contrast to his own wife, Estella-Ruth's grandmother-who was stubborn and headstrong in everything she did. Stunningly beautiful, especially as a young woman, in her prime Laura had been far more enticing, a much greater piece of eye-candy than even her own petite daughter. Where Ruth's breasts were firm and perky, Laura's were large, voluptuous and generous. And Ruth's mother had a sufficiently pretty but compact face, a much different form of beauty than her daughter, who boasted full lips, high cheekbones, and a magnetic smile that made people adore her virtually from the time they first laid eyes on her.

Ruth didn't seem to realize it while growing up, but other contrasts between her mother and grandmother would somehow seem to fashion her own personality. Where Laura remained efficient and methodical, set pretty much in her ways, Grandma Estella lived life as an open book-always exploring new possibilities, while being careful to remain within boundaries society had set in everything from work ethic to attire.

Perhaps sensing that she was similar to her grandmother, far more than to her mother, on most afternoons after school while a pre-teen, Ruth would run over to Grandma Estella's boarding house. There, her grandmother spent many hours teaching her how to make lavish foods, rather than bland, everyday selections such as those that Laura whipped up. Devout in the Mormon Church, her grandfather-Stacy, a meat cutter-faithfully attended services every weekend. Yet Estella rarely attended services, always using the excuse that she was too busy working at their boarding house-which was true. Overall, the family was raised to be faithful and good people, but-as Ruth proclaimed in her interview with Wayne Melton—"nobody was overly religious."

It was during those pre-teen years, before she became close with Virgil, that Ruth was stricken by fantasies that enrapture many young girls-those of horses. Although she had enjoyed seeing people with such animals in Winnemucca, Ruth's first experiences with them came each summer starting at age six. That's when her family first sent her-alone-on a bus trip to visit her Aunt Grace and Uncle Clifford on their ranch in Littlefield, Ariz. Nearly 70 years after that first bus trip while traveling alone at age 6, a journey of more than 1,000 miles, Ruth vividly recalled that it was an innocent time. Parents, at least those from rural communities, would have few worries when putting even their smallest children-at least those of age 5 or better-on buses for major cross-country excursions. It seems people were much more self reliant and trusting then, a sharp contrast to the late 1900s and early 2000s, when the mere notion of having a child travel alone under such conditions was considered downright criminal and dangerous.

As Ruth recalled, her Uncle Clifford was a tall, handsome horseman who labored hard to care for his wife and many children. During summers, especially when Ruth visited, they would all sleep outside since it was far too hot to stay indoors. As she matured, Ruth-at least to a small degree-fantasized about being the lover of a handsome young man who was proficient with horses. Little did she know that she would soon meet such a young man-and then some-in Virgil Bennett Ballard.

And although she was his sister Joaquina's good friend, as a senior citizen Ruth could remember nothing of Virgil during her years in elementary school. That all changed, almost from the moment she first saw him in high school. "I loved his walk!" Ruth would exclaim in the recorded interview. "He had that cowboy hat of his on all the time, giving him a strong, masculine appearance although he was very young. And even though he was thin as a rail, he was strong and muscular, seeming to having far more strength than any fellow of his size should have. His boots clanked ever-so-slightly on the school hallway floors as he went from class to class between sessions, and his walk-his distinctive, manly gate-that way he moves from side to side-it enraptured me. It didn't take more than a day or so after the first moment I first laid eyes on Virg that I began to think of him-literally-all the time."

Amazingly, though, at the time Virg lacked a steady girlfriend. Certainly, at least from Ruth's perspective, there were plenty of "potential pickins" for him in this regard-for the town was packed with girls and young women of many shapes and sizes, just about all of them-but not all of them-with a certain indefinable country beauty.

Yet one day, innocently, Virg approached her during class change in the hallway, and he said, innocently enough: "may I walk you home after school." This made Ruth's heart flutter, literally, for until that moment she hadn't been sure of whether he knew she existed. That day, although he had a car of his own, he made the long walk of nearly three miles with her. Without them saying so openly, each knew it wouldn't be appropriate for him to be alone with her in a vehicle, at least till such time as they might become "boyfriend and girlfriend."

"It was during that walk, that Virg first told me about his passion for poetry," Ruth said. "He mentioned this matter-of-factly, and I didn't think any big thing of it at the time. But before long, we started passing notes in school-all kinds of love notes, that said things like how much we cared for each other, and of how we hoped to see each other after school. Many of the letters even contained his poems."

In conducting the interview, Melton interrupted Ruth, telling her: "Then, you have a full, entire and complete list of Virgil's poems. You have a list of all those he wrote in high school, and during the years after that?"

"Yes, indeed, I do," she didn't miss a beat. "I'll give you the full list, if you want now, and we can review them."

"No, that's not necessary, at least for now," Melton told her. "I'll go over the entire list when I interview Virg tomorrow, while the tape recorder is rolling."

Right away, Melton continued the interview pursuing other subjects, and I shot up, coming to attention at a stand behind my desk.

"Stop the recording!" I pointed to Motamubi.

"What?" he was stunned, shocked by this interruption.

"We all need to just stop for a brief moment, and realize that we've finally stumbled upon the evidence that we seek," I paused, and turned on my intercom to the secretary. "Beverly, please come into my office, now, and shut the door behind you."

"Is something wrong?" Beverly wondered.

"We're about to get some historically significant details," I told her. "I want you in here to take notes, and to film a Cybo-Movie of us as this revelation occurs, to capture the occasion for all mankind, for all perpetuity."

"Those are mighty strong words, boss. I'll be right there." As promised, Beverly was in the room within moments. I could see from the amazed expressions of the three others who had been in the room with me that there was little doubt that what I had just proclaimed was right on track.

Then, in the moment I directed, Motamubi turned the tape back on.

"During that walk, and in the days and months that followed, I became enraptured with Virg's face–which was breathtaking. He was so handsome, just to look at it made my head spin. Do you see this old photo, I have brought here to show you."

"Yeah, yeah," Melton said to her during the interview. "You're right. You are quite an attractive couple."

"See the belt buckle that Virg is wearing, as we stand hugging each other?" Ruth asked Melton.

"Uh, hummm. It looks quite impressive."

"Well, I'm wearing it now-see?"

"Stop!" Annie yelled. This time it was she, Annie, who stood up. "Stop the recording, now! Please!"

As requested, Motamubi turned off the recording machine again, uttering "why all these interruptions."

"I have the belt buckle!" Annie proclaimed. "I have it in my purse! It was passed down through the generations, for all of Ruth's ancestors-as a remembrance of her love for Virg."

Sure enough, momentarily, Annie displayed a stunning gold-laced silver belt buckle. We passed it around, amazed, each enthralled by this find.

"Do you mind if you continue playing the recording," Motamubi remained as impatient as ever. "Let's get this thing over with, and then we can discuss it in detail."

I gave the okay signal, and Ruth continued her tale. Her words were so vivid, so descriptive, so packed with heart that it felt to me almost as if she was right there in the room with us. After hearing her for the past half hour, I already felt as if she was a long-lost friend of mine. And I suppose just about anyone hearing this recording would feel the same.

"I went with Virg's sister to his house one Saturday morning, and I'll never forget it-a huge breakfast his mother had cooked for all the ranch hands. I had never been to anything like it, before or since. The smells, the sights, the sounds, everything seemed so vivid-everyone was happy, and they worked hard. That was the first time I met Virg's mother and father, and after everyone was done eating, Virg took me for a hayride.

"It was just the two of us. We were both so young, so innocent. It was just assumed that we would be married. It was so natural. No word was every spoken about that, because it was just assumed by the two of us. We never fooled around sexually, or anything like that. The most enticing thing that would happen occurred when he would say things like 'nice pants' as he helped me on or off the wagon. We kissed, and we spoke of our dreams, of living together on our own ranch someday. And we knew we would have many children, lots of good children who would look just like the two of us. Virg and I were so in love, so much in love."

"The settings were more romantic than you could ever possibly imagine. He read some to me while on that hayride, and on subsequent hayrides. And the poems . . ." Ruth's words trailed off. The tape continued rolling, but my office and everyone in it remained quiet.

Something had gone wrong, terribly wrong. "What happened!" I barked.

"Darn! Is this tape broken? Is that the end of it? We didn't get to hear what she was going to say! It was getting better and better, just the way I've always dreamed it would be," Annie spoke up.

"It seems like it's a defective tape recording, is that true Motamubi?" Ruby asked. "The tape was only half-way finished. Something has broken, do you think?" "The rest of the tape is blank! Oh, my God! We were just about to get to all the truth!" Motamubi finally couldn't stand it any longer, showing all his emotions. He flipped to the other side of the recording, and it was blank, too.

"These things happen." I observed.

"I'm sorry, so sorry, boss," Motamubi begged for forgiveness.

"There's nothing to forgive," I said, truly meaning what I said. "It's a technical situation."

CHAPTER TWELVE

Frustrated, the five us sat back and stared at each other a few minutes. We all remained quiet. It was as if as a team, collectively, we had nothing to say. The situation spoke for itself, increasing our frustrations. I coughed briefly a few times, on this occasion managing to remain relatively sedate. And rather than weep, as I would have expected her to do in this situation, Annie sat there-seemingly more stoic, brave and fully aware of the situation than First Lady Jacqueline Kennedy had been in October 1963, upon the assassination of her husband. Some people show their true character, their tough inner strength, at the most difficult of times. And I noticed right away that Annie was just one of those people. This apparent damage to the Ruth Lauraene Cracraft Saunders recording would have been enough, it seems, to shatter Annie's dreams. As if a dagger swiping at any chance of happiness, on the verge of when it was about to occur, the recording had broken down at precisely the most horrendous time possible. Along with the death of my wife, and the loss of my girlfriend from high school, I'd had to say this was among the top tragedies of my life.

Yet at least in this instance, there remained hope that a plausible solution could be found. After all, the tape recording label Virgil Ballard, recorded Jan. 11, 2003, was right there in my office. All we needed to do was play it, and hope that it hadn't suffered similar damage, possibly due to water that had seeped into the former elementary school's cornerstone during the past century. "Let's play the Virgil Ballard tape, okay Motamubi?" I inquired. "Are you game?"

"Sure, let's give it a whack."

Everyone present seemed in full agreement, so Motamubi popped that tape into the machine, and clicked the "play" button.

"This is Wayne Melton, . . ." that tape began, "and today is January 11, 2003. I'm here today to interview Virgil Ballard about his relationship with Ruth, and to extensively review the many hundreds of poems he has written through the years. Mister Ballard, I know I often start off with some pretty 'different' type of questions, and this is not to throw you off. Let me begin by asking, please, what is the most bizarre thing that's ever happened to you in your life?"

"Well, what do you mean by strange or interesting? My life has been pretty humdrum, despite all the many great things people say I've done in the real estate industry, and in my personal life. But I'd guess I'd have to say one of the most interesting stories I can remember occurred when I was a kid, in about the fifth grade. It was August 1937, and I accompanied my father, Joaquin Ballard, and my grandfather, JJ Ballard, on a cattle drive-a 200-mile stretch from McDermitt, Nevada, southward through rough high desert terrain to our new Sonoma ranch in Winnemucca.

"There were quite a few hands, real cowboys helping us out, and I'd get up before sunrise each morning for about 10 full days during that trip. We'd always have a good breakfast before the sun rose, and we wouldn't eat again till we got to our destinations at night. Being young, just a boy really, I always brought up the rear, behind the entire heard, while my dad rode near the front pointing the herd, sometimes two or three miles from the drags as we called it. He lead the drive every step of the way.

"Exhausted each night, we all sat by huge campfires. Those were my first experiences at cowboy poetry. The cowboys, including my dad and my grandpa, told poems, some that they had written in their heads that day along the trail drive-or those that they had heard from other cowboys they had met through the years. That's when I learned the art of storytelling, and the meaning of stringing out a good yarn, something I came to appreciate, and a process I appreciate and practice on my own to this day.

"My biggest, brightest memory from that trip is of a man named Big Jim Calhoun, so large and so tall that we all swore that when his time came to meet his maker-we'd all have to find a grand piano case to bury him in. Big Jim's mustache was bigger than a squirrel, at least judging by the way it wiggled above his lips whenever he spoke. Both ends of his mustache were curled so long, so fine, and so circular you could have fit silver dollar coins into them.

"And then, one night, on a day I was particularly tired, I fell fast asleep before the men even started rattling their poems. Laughter awakened me, some sort of joke that had them all laughing like hyenas in the wild, and I realized it was Big Jim's turn to say his peace. This time, he rattled off a verse that I knew I never would forget, a tale about him loving a woman who got away, and died on him, and how nothing after that ever seemed worth anything much at all to him.

"Well, maybe because it was so darn quiet out there on the trail, with not a soul in sight but the cattle and cowboys far up ahead of me, I started writing poems in my head that week, too. I told myself that I was going to find me a good, pretty, healthy gal some day that I could hitch up with, and that I was going to take good care of her, and that we were going to have a big family loaded with a fine bunch of sons.

"And I've got that poem right here, Wayne, would like me to read it to you?" "Sure," Melton answered, sounding genuinely appreciative. "Well, I call it the . . ."

Suddenly, unexpectedly, the voice trailed off. Static began to echo from the machine. Scratchy noises prevailed.

"Holy cow, here we go again," Motamubi said. "What a loss, what a horrible loss this would be to the world if this tape is as broken and decayed as that other one."

Sure enough, Motamubi fast-forwarded to several sections of the tape, where he would always stop it before checking in the "play" mode-only to get that scratchy sound.

This time, it was Ruby who broke out in tears. Tough Ruby. Never-say-die Ruby. Yes, the same Ruby who never in all my years of knowing her had ever shown any sign of weakness. For my part, I coughed a few times, as Annie fetched a load of tissue from my desktop to give to Ruby, who wept so much it seems she forgot to act embarrassed at all for doing this in front of me.

"I can't help it, boss," Ruby revealed her heart's sensations. "What a loss. We were so close."

"Who says we've failed?" I interjected, walking around my desk, and then starting to fiddle with the recording machine along with Motamubi. "Listen, everyone. There is a solution, you know. You might remember from your history books that scientists in a span from 2002 to 2005 finally managed to reveal the contents of what had been called the "18 minute gap" in a White House tape recording from the Nixon administration in 1972. Revelations of what had been in that section of the erased tape rocked the political foundations of Washington, even 30 years after that recording was originally made.

"Well, I'd have to argue, to urge you to remember that that same exact technology, the ability to ferret out hidden or broken information from damaged magnetic tape recordings still exists today-at least the written record of the technology of how to do it exists somewhere. And although there is no need for such technology today, since those types of recording devices are no longer used, I'm sure such a decoding machine can be fixed up or built, in order to help us solve this mystery . . ."

"Great!" Ruby finally perked up, pausing a moment to blow her nose.

And as if suddenly struck by a newfound idea, Motamubi rushed to a container on the floor by my desk, and he picked it up. He then set it on my desk, and used his eager hands to fish through it before quickly pulling out a large envelope labeled "poem."

"Boss, want me to open it?"

"Rip away. We've got nothing to lose."

Within seconds, he handed me a single poem, written in the same distinctive handwriting I recognized as being Virgil Ballard's. Without waiting for a single moment of reflection, I began to read it aloud.

A LONG LONG TRAIL

Close your eyes and hear me tell
Of an ancient love that never fell
Sixty years their chances seemed doomed
When out of the dust a flower bloomed
Sixty years with no contact ever made
Who would have believed their love refused
to fade
She was a beautiful girl full of charm
He a quiet boy right off the farm
A perfect match everyone could tell
'till the old woman from the north cast a spell
Then their connection was torn asunder
With flashes of lightning and claps of thunder
Not even a letter was allowed to pass
No cruder fate could ever surpass
The years dragged by slowly one by one
She grew to be gorgeous and always fun
They each married others as time went by
Raised families but in secret often would cry
Life went on and sure didn't seem fair
The feeling of true love just wasn't there
She never gave up her secret life it seems
Continually searching for the man of her dreams
Sixty years is a mighty long time by rights
It translates into twenty two thousand days and nights
But the roots stayed alive, that flower has bloomed
The spell has withered and died it can be assumed

This couple now talk on a regular basis
Amidst the tedium of living, they are a thriving oasis
Their previous commitments are still in control
But compared to the past they are now on a roll
The chance for their future really looks bright
Though older and slower, they still can excite
In spite of the long long trail back to the past
If it's meant to be, true love will last

Upon finishing this, I looked, and right away I noticed that in that very moment Annie fainted dead-away onto the floor.

No longer crying and still sitting in her chair, Ruby hung her mouth wide open as if it were a tunnel big enough to accommodate a train on its tracks. And along with Beverly, Motamubi knelt on the floor in a feverish effort to revive the heir to what undoubtedly would soon be hailed as the Newfound Ballard Poem Collection.

CHAPTER THIRTEEN

The moment I got home from work that evening, I lay down on the living room couch as my fever soared. I began to cough, although much more gently than this morning. I briefly entertained the notion that perhaps I was becoming a candidate to participate in the United States Life Lottery, which poor Carolina had been among the many who "lost" in the last drawing. I began wondering why I've gotten sick, what I might have done wrong. Certainly, I hadn't been taking good care of myself the previous six months or so. February through May of this year were spent worry about and caring for Carolina, followed the last few months by this internationally acclaimed Ballard historical research, and all the pressure that resulted.

Actually worried that I was catching life threatening pneumonia, I phoned my physician, Dr. Plumas Smirnoff. Five minutes after I left a message at his answering service, he phoned back. Rather than inquiring about my health, though, the first question he asked was: "What's this I see on the news tonight, about your cracking the Ballard case?"

"We haven't solved anything," I said, amid coughing. "My office has made no announcement."

"No?" Smirnoff sounded genuinely concerned about the issue. "Well, I saw an interview with an Annie Something-or-other, I don't remember her name, and she told reporters at a news conference that in your office, she had witnessed unequivocal evidence."

"That's not true," I said, going on further to explain that we had stumbled across plenty of interesting and historical details, but that nothing had been pinned down as far as the origin of the "Looking Back" poem.

The physician then inquired about my general symptoms, and then he requested that I yank the earphone from my ears-and then briefly hold it to my chest for a few moments. Then, I reinserted the communication device in my ear.

"Poor guy," he said. "You do need some medicine. You have pneumonia, a temperature of 102 point seven, and the beginnings of a potential lifelong heart murmur."

"Doctor, am I going to die tonight, or can I go to work tomorrow morning?"

"Funny, funny, Ben. You've always been a jokester. I'll have some additional antibiotics sent over to your place. They should be there in about two minutes. With luck, you should be feeling better by morning. If not, if you're still feeling ill then, and even if you're not, my friend-I want you to take the next few weeks off from work to rest." "Sure thing. Thank you, doctor. Bye."

As soon as we hung up, I realized that I had been lying through my teeth. The last thing I'd ever do is avoid going to work, even though I hated my job with a passion. It's sort of a paradoxical thing, I realize, hating your job with all your heart and soul-all the while having such dedication and passion that you feel a need to work at it, till your dying day.

As soon as the Pharmaceutical Robot arrived at my front door, I punched in the appropriate Dollar-Max amount, and received a canister of the appropriate doses.

The strange thing is, I said "goodbye" to the machine, although it's a Pure-Robot and it doesn't even hear. Momentarily, I sat back down on the living room couch, and drank my first dose-just as I noticed a stack of that day's mail beside me. I realized that I had felt so rotten upon my return home, I failed to remember that I had brought in the mail. I'm old fashioned, in that I register to receive actual pieces of paper in my mail, rather than getting all my deliveries over the Cyber-Net.

Atop the papers, I noticed an envelope from my high school class, Freemont High of 2044. While coughing, I ripped it open to rediscover what I had already expected, we would soon be having our 35-year class reunion. This was just another reminder of that. Within two minutes of opening the envelope, I filled out the form, disc-dropped into my computer, and blasted it via Z-mail to the event organizers. There was no way I would miss that gathering, even if I remained super-ill then, for I kept thinking about my old girlfriend, Patty Carnahan. I actually haven't stopped thinking about her, not a day has passed these many years that I haven't at least briefly-and in some cases for several minutes or hours-thought about what it would be like to be with her, to spend an hour, an afternoon, or even longer.

Perhaps because my initial medicine dose had a bit of a sedative, I lay on the couch and my eyes began to close. I kept thinking about

Virgil Ballard and Ruth Laurene Cracraft Saunders. Somehow, I knew, they had been split apart-perhaps by someone Virg's poem referred to as "the old woman from the north"-and they had just as mysteriously gotten back together. In the case of me and Patty, this "old woman" was undoubtedly fate. And so, I wanted to take fate by the throat, and grasp onto it in order to help take control of my own destiny. I had no fanatical desires about seeing Patty again, I just wanted to meet her, and to talk with her.

I kept thinking this, as I started to dream. First, I saw colorful visions of Virgil and Ruth on the hayride, pulled by horses. I sensed what their words must have been like so long ago, how gentle, how pure, and oh, how innocent. I felt their love, and I knew in my heart that it was real, the kind of love we all yearn for, the kind of love that makes life worth living, and, yes, the kind of love that makes people literally move mountains in order to get what they want. From here, I transitioned into my memories of Patty, of our first kisses, of our delightful times together.

Then, I heard a loud noise. I opened my eyes, to see sunlight streaming through the back doors. "Beep-beep-beep." My brain told me it was the front Door-Blaster, and someone was here for an actual in-person visit. I sat up on the couch, and looked at my watch, realizing it was 9:30 in the morning-the first time in my career that I had been late for work, with my usual reporting time being at 8. Realizing this, I knew with certainty that I must truly be ill.

Cognizant of the fact in-person home visits are rare these days, I stumbled toward the front door. Along the way, I sensed it must be someone from my work, concerned about my well being because I haven't bothered to show up at the office for the first time ever. Upon opening the door, I initially didn't see anyone, and so I figured it must be pranksters running from house to house, ringing Door-Blasters. Seconds later, though, I realized two children stood on the front porch, a boy of about 8 years old and a girl about 10. They both had friendly expressions.

"Our grandpa wants you to come over to our house to visit him," the little girl said. "He says it's urgent that you see him."

"Who are you?" I asked, while coughing slightly.

"I'm Grace Ballard Fegley, and this is my brother, Bennett Ballard Fegley."

"You are Ballards? Ancestors of Wes Ballard, the famous poet."

"Virgil Ballard was our great-great-grandpa," the boy said. "Please come over to our grandpa's house, and visit him. Can you do that? This afternoon? Is that okay?"

"Well, I . . . I've been a little under the weather, and . . ."

"Here's the address," the little girl said, as she handed me a card.

I looked at it, and noticed right away that at 335 Tucker Road is in South Reno, in a community once known as Pleasant Valley.

"Grandpa would like you there at noon, for lunch, and to talk with him."

"Well, I'll try."

"Can I tell him you'll be there?" Grace said, her face compact, sweet, and adorable.

Seeing her youthful, positive expression capped off by all that cuteness, I suddenly realized that had been the name of Virgil and Wes Ballard's mother, Grace. "What is your grandpa's name?"

"Wesley Ballard Fegley. We call him Grandpa Wes."

"Tell your grandpa that God willing, I will be there."

That said, the children scurried back toward the street, each waving back at me, and saying "thank you!" and I felt grateful that at least some children seem happy in this world-most of them apparently failing to realize that life will surely become much more difficult when they reach their adult years-despite all the so-called conveniences of modern gadgetry.

The moment I closed the door, and stepped back into the living room, I realized I was short of breath. I would try to breathe, but my lungs refused to cooperate. Is this what asthmatics feel like? I wasn't wheezy, but sensed that an oxygen machine would have done me a world of wonders. Right away, while heading toward the bathroom, I began to wonder why no one from my work had called. As soon as I got to the bathroom, I phoned my secretary.

"Beverly, I will not be in to work today."

"Boss, that's obvious. We all knew that, from your terrible cough yesterday. For heaven's sakes, stay home and take care of yourself."

"Okay," I answered, trying to sound humbled, but realizing that I've been doing a bit of lying lately, which is totally out of character for me. At that point, I just sensed it would have been better for me to avoid making a big fuss about visiting Wes Bennett Fegley, rather than inform my staff at this point of what's underway. "Is everything all right in the office?"

"Nothing that we wouldn't have expected today. There are more than 100 press trucks outside our office, after that news leak from last night. It seems the whole world wants this story, but they're getting it all wrong, and there . . ."

"I know, then I suppose Ann Breen is keeping them at bay for us?"

"Ann is excellent, the best public information officer you could have possibly hired for your staff, sir. But even a crackerjack public relations person like her can't keep those snot-nosed journalists at bay, no matter how happy that would make us all."

I suggested to Beverly that she ask Ann to simply issue an announcement that last evening's news leaks were unfounded, and that the public can be assured that our office is still looking into the matter of the "Looking Back" poem's origin. Once I finished talking with Beverly, I set about the task of trying to bathe-a long, arduous effort considering my precarious health. Even with all this heated controversy that's erupting, I knew I would have been much happier that moment if I hadn't felt so darn sick.

CHAPTER FOURTEEN

Loaded up on as many pharmaceuticals as my prescriptions would allow, I headed out my front door and began the short walk toward the SkyTube entrance. Within two minutes, I would be at the house in the former Pleasant Valley, which is just 15 miles north of my Carson City home. Exhausted, I hoped that this meeting wouldn't take more than a few hours. Every fiber of my being told me that I needed to get home, and tuck myself into bed for much needed recuperation. My worst fear for the moment was that by exerting myself too much in this excursion I would exacerbate my symptoms, putting myself into a critical condition that would be difficult-if not impossible-to escape.

So, I walked as slowly, as steadily as possible. About halfway from my home to the SkyTube, my earphone bleeped. I answered, worried that it might be important news from my office: "Hello."

"Is this Ben Rivera, the State Archivist?"

"It is. How may I help you? Who's calling?"

"Opie Russell."

"The famous movie star?"

"That's right. I want to talk to you about all this historical research you're trying to pull."

"Trying to pull? What do you mean? My office is simply doing methodical, detailed, and well-thought research."

"Why can't you people leave history alone? You're ruining things."

"How am I ruining things? Are you talking about "Looking Back," that romantic movie, the movie in which you portray Wes Ballard? How in the world could this research ruin it all for you? That movie was made more than three years ago."

"Residuals, man, residuals. My biggest income from that job, through my contract, is from residuals. Film rentals, and replays on Cyber-TV are where the big bucks are at."

"I've read in the news, mister, that you're selfish. Is it true? Are you actually asking me to rewrite history, to censor history for your..." I began to cough, nonstop.

"People are going to stop seeing the movie, they're going to lose interest if you prove that Wes Ballard never wrote that poem."

I kept coughing, as the world-famous actor continued rattling. Finally, I interrupted, saying: "Give me a break. How dare you make such a demand." "I have rights, sir, and ..."

Unwilling to hear much more of this jerk, I arrived at the Sky Tube entrance, deposited my Dollar-MAX card, and stepped inside the cylinder.

"Sorry," I said, while punching in my destination coordinates to Pleasant Valley. "You can take your acting career, and stuff it. People find greater satisfaction in the truth, than they do in lies like yours-that rob them of any chance for happiness, of honestly knowing their true heritage ... Bye."

CHAPTER FIFTEEN

Relaxed and at ease despite my serious illness, I hobbled off the SkyTube at the intersection of Pleasant Valley Drive and NR-1, formerly known as U.S. Highway 395. This was the closest intersection to the Wes Ballard Fegley home, which was nearly one-quarter mile up a hilly area. I cursed myself for not bringing a walking cane, which I don't normally need. Yet due to my illness, I found it increasingly difficult to walk-and the small hill up ahead made me think of Mount Everest. Goodness knows, I hoped a little fresh air would do me a world of good. But after strolling up Pleasant Valley Drive nearly a half block, I thought I would faint. Rather than risk falling flat on my face, I sat at the edge of the road. Thankfully, I had remembered to bring my medication, which I took-swallowing it without the benefit of beverages. Hopefully, I thought, this medicine would eliminate a persistent difficulty in breathing, uncomfortable sensations that seemed to intensify with each passing minute.

To my good fortune, I looked up to see those frisky children, Grace and Bennett running down the hill toward me. They pushed a wheelchair, one of those old fashioned kind that didn't have a 25 mile-per-hour engine.

"You look like Abraham Lincoln," Grace said, right when they got to me. "The resemblance is kind of interesting, sort of funny and amazing. Why are you sitting down?"

"Oh, just thought I'd take in a little bit of this fantastic view," I uttered the first answer that came to my head. All the while, I thought how mature and observant this little girl was, for she verbalized her observation about my appearance with far more eloquence than most adults.

"Grandpa is excited that you're coming to our house," Bennett said, while pulling at my right hand in order to help me stand. "We saw you through the binoculars. Grandpa thinks it's funny."

"He thinks what is funny?" I said, curious but not angry. "Hasn't he ever seen a man sit by the side of a road?"

"Grandpa thinks you look like Lincoln," Grace said, pointing toward the wheelchair seat. "Please sit down here. I have a surprise for you."

"A surprise?" I inquired, while immediately accepting her offer to sit in the chair. I'm not too proud to admit when a little assistance might carry me a long way. "What surprise?"

Momentarily, Bennett pulled a large black stovepipe hat out from a compartment under the seat. He handed me the hat, and as naturally as if I might have worn one every day, the universe motivated me to immediately put it on. "Wow!" Grace said, while turning the wheelchair in the uphill direction, toward Ames Lane, about five houses up. "That goatee you have makes you look even more like that president than the actors I've seen playing him on Cyber-TV." Struck by a sudden chill, my only thought was to get into the warmth of their Grandpa's house as soon as possible. Within seconds, Grace flicked on a battery powered engine, and I steered the wheelchair uphill-as both children stood on a small perch at the back. I'd guess we went a respectable speed of about 7 miles per hour, a pretty good clip compared to my current walking standards. "The sooner we get there, the better," I thought. "This isn't so bad."

"Go right. Right! Right!" the children cheered, and I did just that, heading up Ames Lane. I looked at small ranch-style homes on both sides of the street and realized with great delight that some of the properties even had horses-now an endangered species, and not abundant with plenty of livestock as they had been in the 1900s.

"Left! Left! Go left!" the children cheered, as we arrived at Cooke Drive. I obediently followed their instructions, and headed up that street, amazed that this one tiny old, antiquated engine could haul the three of us with ease. Before I knew it, we turned right onto Tucker Road, and it was the first house on the left-a small structure. In the back of it, a fence crawled up a hill, surrounding a property of probably less than one acre. Right in the middle of the gravel driveway, an old man stood-using the support of a crooked wood cane with a silver colored handle-just the type of contraption I wanted at that moment. The man stared right at me. He had the makings of mischievous smile. He seemed to try to make a poker face, which he failed miserably at doing.

"Mister, you've made my day," he said, approaching to shake my hand as the wheelchair came to a stop. "Welcome to the estate of the late Virgil Bennett Ballard."

Dumbfounded, I stepped out of the wheelchair, and for some reason that I couldn't quite explain I suddenly felt much better. My breathing was no longer labored, and I even surprised myself by issuing a broad smile.

"You must be Wesley Ballard Fegley," I said, offering my hand as a sign of friendship. As we shook hands, I realized this gent of perhaps 65 years old was much stronger than he appeared, his forearms more like those of a weightlifter than those of a maturing gentleman. He wore muddy boots, jeans and a cowboy shirt, which made me think of what authentic Western men must have looked like long ago. He also wore the distinctive ring of a mason, just as his own great-grandfather had been.

"Come right on in, and set a piece," Wesley said. "We've got quite a bit of talking to do."

Before long, we strolled through the front door and into the small home-which Wesley explained was in pretty much the same condition as it had been when Virgil bought it the early 1970s. A few pieces of furniture were even original to that era, and a rocking chair by the fireplace was even older than that. As Wesley stood by the chair, and using his wrinkled right hand to rock it back and forth a bit, he explained that his great-great-great-great grandfather, JJ Ballard—enshrined in an oil painting hung above the fireplace-had owned the chair.

"Then, Virgil Ballard was your great-great-grandfather?" I asked, eager to get as much detail as possible. More than ever, I was filled with curiosity as to why I had been summoned. What new, interesting detail did this man want to give me-if any?

"My grandfather on that side of the family tree was Jonathan Fegley-and my grandmother was his wife, Kelli Ballard. My grandma Kelli was Virgil Ballard's granddaughter, and her own father was Wesley Ballard-who owned a successful and widely acclaimed comic book store."

"You mean, your grandmother's father was Wesley Ballard, the famous poet killed in the automobile accident outside of Winnemucca?"

"Not quite," Wesley Ballard Fegley said, as he sat down in the rocking chair. "You see, there were-or are-three Wesleys, and each of us had the nickname of 'Wes.' The first was the gentleman killed in the wreck. That was, as you probably know, Virgil's younger brother, about nine years his junior. The second Wesley was Wesley Curtis Ballard, the son of Virgil-who named that child in honor of his deceased brother. And my grandmother Kelli, had heard all of these stories-so that's how I got my name."

"Oh, I see. It's all pretty basic, really," I gave an honest observation. "Do you mind if I sit down?"

"Excuse me. I should have offered right away," he said, motioning for me to sit in a couch opposite his rocking chair. "By all means, make yourself feel at home."

"Then, you knew your Grandma Kelli? She spoke of her grandfather, Virgil?"

Just then, a woman entered the room. Since I'm always courteous and polite, my first inclination was to stand and offer a greeting. Yet still weakened by my illness, I stayed put-and Wesley Bennett Fegley summarily announced that, "I'd like you to meet my wife, Doreen. . . . This is the State Archivist, darling, Mister Rivera."

"Hi, Abraham," she said, giggling just a bit as she reached to shake my hand. "I'm sorry. I can't help it. It's just that you look so great in that outfit . . . Would you like coffee, milk, anything to drink?"

"Do you have hot chocolate? That sounds like just the thing that could warm me up?"

"Certainly. And would you like a sandwich?"

"Whatever you dish up is fine with me."

She said "fine" and left to an adjoining kitchen, as I coughed a few times.

"Sounds like you're a bit under the weather," Wesley observed. "That's why I sent the children down for you with the wheelchair. I could see that from a distance. I hope you don't mind taking the assistance."

"Believe me, your gracious help has been appreciated."

"Well, as long as we're discussing it, then, I just thought you would want to know that my mother, Janice, was born in 2010 when my grandma Kelli was 25 years old-and I was born in 2034 when Janice was 24. My father, Martin Fegley, was a soldier during World War III, and in the later years of his life, he worked as a private detective."

"I think it's fantastic that your family has been able to keep this property, and some of the original furniture for all these many years," I said, just then noticing a photograph of Virgil Bennett Ballard, next to a logo for the Ballard Company.

"I see you've noticed Virgil?" Wesley said. "You seem fascinated. Well, I don't blame you, I've been fascinated about this all my life, for a lot longer period than you have."

I told Wesley that I was well aware that the Ballard Company remained vibrant and strong, among the most respected and profitable real estate companies in the West.

"Yeah, I worked there myself, and spent a whole career there."

"Is that why you've asked me here today, to tell me about your family history?"

Wesley paused a moment, and he began to rock back and forth every slowly. That smile that he had tried to hide when I first saw him back on the driveway was now clear, uncensored and vibrant-but also showing what a perceived as distain.

"I just wondered," he said, scratching his chin, "why you or the people on your staff never bothered to try to contact me. Here I'm seeing all this stuff, all these developments in the news media, day after day-and not a single reporter and not a single person from your staff has bothered to ask anything of myself or of my family. Why?"

"Why?" Stunned, I realized that what he observed was true. "I honestly don't have a plausible answer. Sometimes, I suppose, all of us-at one point or another in our lives-fail to check into what we consider the 'obvious' because we just assume things."

"I wish we could have gotten off to a better start here," he said, his smile suddenly gone. The children had darted outside, and through the back window I noticed them playing on a sagebrush-covered hill. "It just irks me, how the government always assumes things about people. It makes me angry and upset." "You have a right to be angry," I gave my honest assessment, as Doreen re-entered the room, carrying a table tray, which she set right in front of me.

"Hope you like this," Doreen said, while pulling a cover off a plate of food, the warm turkey sandwich immediately beckoning me although I wasn't the least bit hungry.

"Serve your husband first." I felt guilty.

"No, you eat," Wesley observed. "Don't argue. Eat to build your energy. Don't wait. Chow down while it's hot."

Rather than argue, I took a bite and realized I still felt a bit too sick to eat much. While dabbling my mouth with a napkin,

I urged Wesley to tell me whatever he wanted about his family's past-especially specifics on the origin of those poems. Doreen returned, and set a tray in front of her husband. Quiet for the first time since we met, Wesley finally started eating, and he didn't say a word.

"I'm all ears," I said, while struggling to take another bite. I decided it wouldn't be wise to show that I really was weak, almost too ill to move.

"Who says I have anything to say?" He paused briefly while eating his sandwich. "Well, sir, you were the one who asked me here."

"Maybe I've said my peace."

Realizing that to play the part of a wimp might not serve my efforts well, I piped up, telling him how sorry I was for the oversight in not seeking him out, and that there was no excuse for such ineptitude. Within a few seconds, I found myself groveling, taking blame, and confessional in nature, a tactic I had never tried in life-at least to any great degree-until that afternoon. But rather than speak only briefly, I used what salesmen call a 'mirror' technique. I became exactly like Wesley, the man across from me. I behaved like him, and actually latched onto his earlier statements-reforming them, as if to make his thoughts my own. I spoke of my own disappointment in government, of how disillusioned I had become with politicians, and how much I dislike bull-shitters who promise the moon when they want to convince you something-and then they end up not doing a blasted thing, or at least very little.

Within a few minutes, Wesley started speaking and smiling again: "Mister Rivera, you're telling me what I want to hear, whether you know it or not, and I like it-because I believe politicians and public officials of many kinds rob us all of ultimate happiness, no matter how close we come to obtaining it."

This time, I was the one who decided to be quiet. I clammed up, once again mirroring the way he had been before.

"You know what, Mister Rivera, I'll have to admit I like you, and that's a pretty hard thing for me to do. I don't like people, most of them anyway."

"I'm on track. I understand, because I'm pretty much the same way." "Then, that means you're tired of all the bureaucratic mumbo-jumbo?" "By all means."

My saying this seemed to be the magic key to opening him up, to the point he was ready to reveal important secrets that I hoped-even prayed-would help put my mind at ease and help conclude my office staff's extensive research into this case. Wesley stood, and he pulled the rocking chair several feet to his left.

"Come here," he said, using his hand to beckon me. "I have something to show you, something I'm sure you'll want to see. It's something guaranteed to spike your interest."

Without saying a word, I stood and took a few steps in that direction. As I did this, he moved a small rug that had been underneath the rocking chair. There, he stuck his finger into a small knot hole, and pulled up a hidden door.

"Oh, wow!" I said, as the secret compartment came into full view. "This is a treasure, isn't it?"

Sure enough, while standing beside him, I looked down into that secret compartment. Inside, was a single white binder, labeled with these words: "The Complete and Unabridged Poems of Virgil Bennett Ballard, 1927-2025."

"I have them all memorized," Wesley said. "All of them. Want to hear me say one?"

Sure, I answered, still in awe of this amazing discovery.

"Then, I'll say it aloud, before I hand you the book," Wesley promised, as his wife re-entered the room-tears welled in her eyes. From that moment, I could tell that all along Doreen had been aware that her husband was going to present this book to me. "The poem is called, 'The Dream Catcher.' Here I go . . ."

THE DREAM CATCHER

> A dream catcher hangs from my bed post
> It catches my dreams, if I may boast
> And weaves them into the fabric of my day
> Many the surprises that appear on this buffet
> Those dreams I really want to catch
> Come by day, they are the best of the batch
> I must carry my dream catcher on my shoulder
> To catch my dreams before they start to smolder

A tear wandered down Doreen Fegley's apple-colored left cheek. And as the poem ended, at the precise moment the great-great-great-great grandchildren of Virgil Ballard bolted into the living room, as they played cowboy's and Indian's. There were no toy arrows or toy guns, only the sound of the youngsters' incessant giggling as I began to cough once again, ever so slightly.

CHAPTER SIXTEEN

Three months later, I lay in my hospital bed at Saint Mary's Regional Medical Center near downtown Reno, 30 miles north of my Carson City home. I had been hospitalized 11 weeks, beginning about a week after I had left the Fegley home that afternoon.

Being bedridden with illness these days is extremely rare, because it seems doctors know how to cure just about everything but certain forms of cancer and the most vicious types of pneumonia, which I had. The nurses did everything they could to keep me bottled up, tied down to the bed. Rest assured, though, that forever feisty and surly, I wasn't about to remain cooped up like a chicken on a conveyor belt. The doctors called my illness pneumonia intermixed with anemia. Instead, I called it "nothing but a nagging cold, laced with my own stupidity." Without question, this is the period when I started to become convinced that, yes indeed, all questions are stupid.

"What's the latest?" some nurses would ask. "Has your staff determined who wrote the famous poem?" and even "Don't you feel weird, not having all the answers, and frustrated that you can't go out there and conduct some of the research yourself?"

It seemed every other question I heard was about Virgil Ballard, or Wesley Ballard, or "isn't it romantic, what people are saying about Ruth? Is it true? What do you think she was like? I've heard she was pretty, even well into her 90s."

These kinds of statements persisted so much, without letup, to the point where I actually began to wonder whether nurses actually worried about me at all. You'd think they could ask me about my symptoms. But no, it's Wesley this, and Virgil that, and isn't that Ruth a princess, and I've seen pictures of their family, and so on, and so forth.

Topping this off, some of the nurses seemed to spy on me, and on several of my key personnel, when I summoned them to my bedside for regular staff meetings. From the reclusive way Ruby and Motamubi behaved when they visited, the nurses all probably thought we worked for the CIA.

Even the governor-that jerk, excuse my English-had popped by for an obligatory visit, but only after ensuring the press was well aware of his plans for that day. Some greasy reporters had even unsuccessfully tried to sneak into my patient room, hoping to get an exclusive interview about the latest findings in the Ballard Case. Well, you'd think the press would be mindful enough to do some research on its own, to come up with an exclusive scoop of some sort about the true facts of history. Instead, they concentrated on the so-called "sexiness" of the moment. In this instant, for some strange reason, that "sexiness" meant me, perhaps because I was terribly ill while investigating a romantic story. It was as if every editor west of the Mississippi, and throughout some foreign countries as well, was telling his reporters to find out everything you can about Ben Rivera. Why, wouldn't you know, word even leaked out to a tabloid that I had three photographs of Ruth and Virgil hung on my hospital room wall. As one might expect, this enraged much of the world, which had come to believe that I had been sacrilegious for defying memories of the beloved poet Wesley Ballard, and his beautiful girlfriend Wilhelmina Perry. At that point, honestly, I had misgivings about whether that couple even actually existed. It seemed I had been just about the only person in the entire world to come to that conclusion.

As if to drive this point home, on one unseasonably cool late August afternoon I sat in my hospital bed-my mouth hooked to one of those newfangled oxygen machines. The doctors had begun trying every trick they knew to rebuild my ravaged lungs, which had been attacked with rolling bouts of pneumonia throughout the summer. Every time I exhaled, the moisture of my breath would fill the green, clear plastic with a fine mist. Out of the corner of my eye, I saw Annie step inside my patient room.

Right away, I closed my eyes, and faked being asleep. Although my office staff had given Annie clearance to visit on occasion, I remained upset with her for leaking incorrect information to the press after we first heard the recordings. I'd rather have spent an entire afternoon with my eyes closed than have to lay eyes on her. The idea of wasting a breath on this woman left me feeling exhausted, for she had taken more out of me spiritually than I ever thought possible of any person.

I'm sure Annie didn't do this intentionally. But the underlying message from her always seemed to ring strong: that I'm a louse for failing to get to the bottom of the Ballard Case when people needed me most. Still, at least Annie cared enough to visit, and to show at least a smattering of genuine concern-asking only about my health, rather than the historical research.

Well, as I lay there, trying to fake Annie out as if I was asleep, she gently took me by the hand and whispered: "Ben, I know you hear me. I worry about you all the time, as a friend. I know you missed your high school reunion last month, and how much you had looked forward to it..."

"How did you know that," I wheezed. Her observation was too pointed to go unanswered.

"Ben, you mumble in your sleep. The first few weeks when you were stuck in this lousy place, when you often went in and out of consciousness, you would mumble about the reunion, and say how you would get better, and go there, so you could see your old girlfriend, Patty Carnahan."

"I did? I said that?"

"You did, you said how much you loved her. And then you went into that coma for two months. Ben, do you remember? Gosh, how you scared us. I've only known you a short while, but you're like a second father-or an uncle-to me. I appreciate..."

"Please go, Annie. I'm embarrassed," I wheezed louder. "I wish that..."

"Ben, I've brought someone special here to see you."

Hearing this, I opened my eyes wide. And then I saw her, standing beside Annie. Right there, before my very eyes, just as beautiful as ever.

There she stood-Patty Carnahan, my old girlfriend, with those huge blue eyes. Patty, with that infectious grin. Patty, there at my bedside, she looked gorgeous and delicious for a woman of her maturity. If I wasn't so darn sick at that point, so blasted weak, I would have sat up and given her a big hug. "Patty. Oh. I don't want you to see me this way."

"It's okay," she said, taking my hand, as Annie moved away and silently disappeared from the room.

"My darling, oh, you look beautiful."

"You look pretty darn cute, too, mister, considering the shape you're in," Patty pulled her fingers through my hair, which I knew must have felt as greasy as an undercooked hamburger. But she didn't seem to mind.

"You came here? How did you find me?"

"I came here, after I saw a news report on your predicament."

"You did?"

"And I met Annie down in the lobby. She's a sweet young woman, and she told me everything about . . ."

"Be wary. She doesn't always get all her details straight."

"Well, I've got plenty of accurate info, which you might find pretty inspiring."

"Accurate details?" I tried to sit up.

"Mister, do you know what you've inspired people all around the world?"

"I have no idea of what you're talking about."

"Word got out, about your theory about your initial findings. You mumble in your sleep you know. And the nurses spread word, about your belief that Ruth and Virgil found each other. That life is too short. That people ignore each other for too long, when they should reach out for each other-especially those they love with all their hearts."

Patty paused, kissed my cheek, and continued: "Ben, the basic story, what you believe about Ruth and Virgil, has become so real, so vivid, that it has inspired many people all around the world-just in the past few months." "But I . . ."

Patty gently put a finger over my mouth, signaling for me to remain quiet: "Long-lost relatives and lovers all around the world-tens of thousands of them, or maybe millions of them, have been reuniting in just these past few months, all because you have inspired them. People around the world are rooting for you to get better. This hospital is being overwhelmed with gifts for you, and flowers for you, and letters for you. Haven't you heard? The stories of Ruth and Virgil are beginning to spread, of how they were separated for all those many years. No one should have to go through that, no one should have to endure what they did-to have missed out so much in life . . . The way you and I missed each other, too."

"Patty, I should have called you."

"I won't say too much, young man. You need to rest. I realize you feel a need to find the truth about what really happened between Ruth and Virgil. And I want you to know that I came here, Ben, to reunite with you. Because I love you, and I've thought of you every day, and my heart has been broken-shattered-not having been with you through all of these years. I'm sorry we weren't together. The story of you, and of what you have found, it has inspired me, just as it has inspired the rest of the world." A tear fell from pretty Patty's face onto my cheek.

She gave me a gentle, sweet kiss, and promised she would return the following morning.

Oblivious to my condition, I turned onto my right side and closed my eyes. In the past five minutes, my dreams had finally come true. There she was, the love of my life. And I began to think that so many people-in many countries, and in many cities-were undergoing similar reunions, similar emotions. All these changes, all these joys, were reaching out to their true loves across the seven oceans, all because of one couple from long ago-or at least the legend of them.

In that moment, my desire to live rekindled. "I want to live," I whispered to myself, and began drifting off to sleep-trying, struggling to convince myself that it hadn't been just a dream, that my pretty Patty truly had been at my side only minutes earlier. With her, I knew, I could finally achieve the happiness that had always somehow eluded me.

CHAPTER SEVENTEEN

Much had changed by seven months later, the following March. Arm-in-arm, Patty and I strolled leisurely in the neighborhood surrounding Saint Mary's Regional Medical Center. My mind was finally at ease, now that my staff had finally deciphered the two tape recordings.

It had taken an amount of Dollar-MAX equal to ten years of my entire department's budget. But the money had been allocated during a special session of the Nevada Legislature for that purpose, at the urging of the governor. The money was used to rebuild a replica of a once-defunct machine that had deciphered the gaps in the old Richard Nixon tapes. That technology had been temporarily obliterated when the original machine had been destroyed in the 2010s, since it was no longer necessary. All damaged magnetic recordings that could be found had already been deciphered, and the technology no longer was needed anyway because all information systems had gradually been replaced by digital systems.

Delighted beyond belief, a week before I took that stroll with Patty, my office staff had played the original recordings in my patient room. And since I had finally become ambulatory, I finally was able to enjoy hearing those tapes right along with them. The delight expressions of Ruby, Motamubi and Beverly will be implanted on my brain till my dying day. Just as important, physicians concluded all that excitement did me a world of good, refreshing my spirit to the point I regained much of what once had been my widely known vigor, a continual spark of vitality. Despite the loss of nearly 70 pounds, I felt my strength gradually return, with each day marking new improvements.

The moment the tapes finished playing, I authorized our public information officer, Ann Breen, to release digital versions of the recordings in their entirety to the news media. Word soon spread to every corner of the globe of the "robbery" that had occurred, the theft of the companionship between Ruth and Virgil.

With great certainty and clarity, in their separate interviews these lovers disclosed that it wasn't until more than 50 years after they separated that they realized what had happened. When Ruth was 15, her grandmother, had encouraged her to move from Winnemucca to Salt Lake City to take a two-year course at a beautician school. Ruth agreed, but only after receiving a job offer at a Winnemucca hair salon and a promise from her family that she would be able to return there after she graduated.

At first, Virgil balked at the plan, since the notion of being away from Ruth pulled at his heart. The idea of being away from her for a single day, let along a few years, left him crushed and disappointed. Yet he finally agreed, convinced that they would be able to marry immediately upon her return, get a ranch of their own, and start a family.

As planned, the couple wrote each other daily for six months, passionate love letters-and poems by Virgil-that spoke of their undying passions for one another. But then, one day, without warning, the letters stopped crossing through the mails. Since it was his job in the Ballard family to check its postal box in town every few days, Virgil always left the Post Office disappointed. Still, faithfully, as deeply in love as ever, he continued to send letters-but none were ever answered. Meanwhile, in Salt Lake City, where Ruth lived in a boarding house owned and operated by her grandmother, she would return home from beauty school each day only to find that letters from Virgil had stopped coming. Grandma Estella had been in charge of getting and posting the mail each day, and Ruth had no reason at the time to question or suspect a problem on her end.

Still, both Virgil and Ruth continued sending each other letters, which were never received. Finally, after about four months of not receiving replies, each of them stopped sending letters.

"I rode my horse up into the mountains, and spent the day alone, weeping," Virgil revealed in his recorded interview. "I cried, for I sensed that this woman of my life, this gorgeous gal that made life worth living-who seemed to make the universe itself shine in every glorious way possible-she must have been taken from me, that she must have fallen in love with someone else."

Ruth had a similar reaction, for she had no interest at all in other men. The years passed, and as people do through the course of their lives, Ruth and Virgil met and married other people and started families. Virgil proved to be a strong and good father for his children, Rand, James, Wesley, three men who went on to have successful professional careers, and Tracy, who died as a young woman in a tragic overdose of medications. His youngest daughter was Cary Samara Ballard, the only child from his marriage to Caryl. And of course, as we had already discovered, the great prides of Ruth's life were her daughters Laura Louise, Kathleen Ruth, Marsha Lynn, Stacie Rae, and Holly Ann-the great-grandmother of Annie.

Despite those joys in having their separate families, Ruth and Virgil thought of each other often through the years. During the 1950s, 1960s, 1970s, 1980s, and 1990s, each awakened in sleepless nights, thinking of each other, yearning for each other. The pair never laid eyes on each other till they attended a Winnemucca High School reunion with their respective spouses in 1995.

Upon seeing Virgil leave the Red Lyon Hotel in Winnemucca as that year's reunion ended, Ruth broke down into a sea of tears. She had yearned to speak in depth with him, to share her dreams, to tell him of everything that had transpired in her life the previous half century. Yet since they were with their spouses, and due to the way conversations flowed, Ruth and Virgil never were able to express the strong feelings they still felt for each other.

It wasn't until the next reunion in 2000 that they began to discuss at least some of what had happened. At first, each blamed the other for ceasing their letters so long ago. But each honestly swore that they continued the letter-writing campaign, after letters stopped from the other. Upon sharing these details, together they reached the only possible conclusion.

Ruth's grandmother had stopped posting letters Ruth had tried to mail to Virgil. And when his letters would arrive in Salt Lake City for Ruth, her grandmother would also either hide them or throw them away.

MAIL CALL

I STOOD IN BACK AT MAIL CALL
HOPING THEY MIGHT CALL MY NAME
OTHER MEN OPENED THEIR LETTERS
BUT FOR ME IT WAS ALWAYS THE SAME

I TRIED TO HIDE MY FEELINGS
AS I SHRUGED AND TURNED AWAY
I WAS TOO MACHO TO SHOW I CARED
BUT THE HURT WAS THERE TO STAY

THEY SAY HOPE SPRINGS ETERNAL
AND I KNOW THAT TO BE TRUE
EVEN WHEN YOU KNOW ITS OVER
AND HOPING MAKES YOU BLUE

YEARS PASSED SLOWLY, 20, 40, 50 AND MORE
ONE DAY I GOT A LETTER THOUGH
WITH HER NAME THERE IN THE CORNER
AS I HELD IT, MY OLD HANDS TREMBLED SO
THEN CASTING MY EYES UPWARD
A PRAYER WAS IN MY HEART
SO BITTER SWEET MY FEELINGS
SO MANY LONG YEARS APART
EVER SO SLOWLY I OPENED IT
THOUGH I COULD BARELY SEE
TEARS BLURRED MY EYESIGHT
NO LONGER THE MACHO ME SHE SIGNED
IT "LOVE" I SAW

ALL REASON QUICKLY LEFT ME
OLD DEFENSES BEGAN TO THAW
NOW I'M SURE THAT PEOPLE WONDER
WHY I HAVE A SECRET SMILE
GOD LAID HIS HAND UPON ME
I CAN CALL HER MINE FOR AWHILE

It was as if word of this discovery shot a bullet straight through the hearts of Ruth and Virgil. Unaware of what Grandma Estella had done, as teens they each were overcome with melancholy. For each, this sadness persisted, both pining for the years, for the times that might have been. Way back when they became young adults, Grandma Estella had found what she considered a suitable husband for Ruth.

But Ruth found another man-George, and she ended up caring for him, taking care of him in every good way she knew how as he worked hard at a variety of jobs to support their family. Before marrying George, Ruth had the opportunity to meet her biological father, Francis LeRoy Cracraft, for whom she had pined for as a child. That meeting came in 1948 in Salt Lake City, where Ruth's mother had taken her to visit him-after learning he had returned home after serving in World War II.

Francis broke down in tears and hugged his teen-aged daughter, when they first saw each other on a street near downtown Salt Lake City. And her father also hugged his ex-wife, Ruth's mother, Laura, telling her she looked more beautiful than ever. Along with Laura, Ruth spent that afternoon visiting him at his mother's home in that community. Finally, with the help of her mom, Ruth had rekindled the relationship with her dad-which she felt would make her more fulfilled, giving her a greater sense of happiness.

But that didn't last long, because just one year later, at age 40, Cracraft died in a Salt Lake City hospital of a spinal infection sustained when left for dead on a South Pacific battlefield a few years earlier.

Not long after that, living a separate life from Ruth, Virgil got drafted into the U.S. Army to serve during the Korean War. He had been drafted two times earlier, but on those occasions had been rejected for admission due to what physicians described as an infection in his blood. The third time proved to be the charm, though, and Virgil spent the duration of his enlistment at a military base in Pennsylvania, where he met and married the mother of his children. Claudette was his second wife, for he had been briefly married to a woman, Jasmine, in the late 1940s while attending the University of Nevada in Reno.

Not long after leaving the military, in the early 1950s Virgil and Claudette lived briefly at a ranch home he built in Fallon, a rural community in west central Nevada. An electrical malfunction ignited a fire that gutted that residence on July 28, 1955, destroying all worldly possessions they owned, except the clothes they happened to wear at the time. As luck would have it, that day Virgil had been wearing his cherished belt buckle. Everyone escaped injury, at least of a physical nature.

As the decades passed, and Ruth and Virgil pined for each other, she worked hard building a reputation as a successful beauty shop owner in Salt Lake City, and he labored at several jobs while slowly building a successful career as a real estate agent. He eventually founded the Ballard Company Inc., a real estate sales firm that gradually grew to a successful and popular operation.

Virgil and Claudette divorced in October 1968, and he stayed married to his third wife, Caryl who died of breast cancer shortly after the reunion in 2000. In responding to a condolence card that Ruth had sent, Virgil wrote this one phrase: "I think of you often."

Those simple words, that one sentence, helped rekindle their communication-which grew and intensified. Before long, they started visiting with each other at least every several months. Ruth's husband, George, by then in his early 80s, depended on her for her constant love and the good care she provided him. Then, one day, Virgil gave Ruth a surprise gift, the belt buckle he had acquired through a catalogue so many years ago-which he had spent an entire month's of his earnings to get. Fondly, they remembered those times, which had been shattered by the death of his younger brother, Wesley, in that tragic auto accident. For the first time, during the recorded interview, Virgil was able to give the basics of that horrific wreck. Alone, Wesley had been driving a car on old U.S. Highway 40 just outside of Winnemucca, when a giant hauling truck crossed into his lane-hitting him head-on, and killing him instantly.

Each still carrying fond memories of Virgil's brother, Ruth and Virgil began to share the many poems he had written-many penned after their relationship reignited.

Most of those poems comprise the book that Wesley Bennett Fegley, his great-great-grandson, had given me the previous summer after hoisting it from the secret compartment in his living room floor. With Mister Fegley's blessing, my office released that collection of poems to the public last summer.

The poems, hailed as the "Virgil Bennett Ballard Collection" became an immediate international best seller-the biggest single seller in Amazon.com history. "What about that final mystery?" Patty asked me, amid our stroll. "People still wonder who wrote the most famous poem, 'Looking Back.'" "They never mention in the recording-specifically-who wrote it, did they?" I observed. "It's a question I think I can solve, along with the mystery-indeed, if that's the case-of how the world came to believe Virgil's brother wrote it." Patty and I continued the rest of our walk in silence, neither saying a word. We had shared so much with each other in the previous eight months that our hearts beat as one. Thankfully, this is true: the poems of Virgil Ballard had brought us together, just as they had molded so many people around the world as one. For the sake of my own newfound peace of mind, I only hoped it would continue to last.

CHAPTER EIGHTEEN

Two years later, at this year's spring gathering of the American Association of State Archivists in Denver, members converged amid the first major controversy in our organization's history. A week before the event, Washington Post columnist Pierce McMullen began lobbying for my ouster from our group's presidency, although I was running unopposed for a third consecutive two-year term.

"Ben Rivera has disgraced historians everywhere through his shoddy research practices, and his antiquated methods which are best described as dismal," McMullen wrote. "He gained international fame in the Virgil Ballard case. Whoever held the State Archivist job in Nevada when those discoveries were made would have gained fame. But rather than focus most of the attention on the Ballard family, and on the poetry, Mister Rivera has been shameless in promoting himself-especially his new book,

'American Archivist,' which has been a nationwide bestseller the past three weeks."

Although irritated by the assessment, I arrived at the Denver Hilton, fully intending to go ahead with my candidacy-no matter what misinformed journalists might believe. With Patty at my side as my new wife, upon my arrival I strolled with her through the Hilton lobby, feeling more healthy and energetic than when we dated in high school.

The first two days of the three-day event blasted by fast, as members learned everything from the new technique of using cyber-based fingerprints to track family heritage-to methods of dealing with the press after it disseminates misinformation regarding the past. Finally, on the third day, the international media converged in the banquet room. Journalists knew ballots would be placed immediately after the luncheon, during which I was to give my formal address as president-followed by my brief campaign speech as the only candidate.

Right on queue, a surprise guest appeared. I had helped arrange his appearance, although the media and the membership had not been informed. The association secretary, Malcolm Culbertson of Tennessee, approached the podium as a chocolate cake desert was served, and made this announcement: "Ladies and gentlemen, I present to you the man who will introduce today's speaker. For the introduction, please welcome Oscar-winning actor Opie Russell."

Wild cheers erupted amid a standing ovation. Everyone got caught by surprise, especially the women-virtually all of them delighted and even enthralled to feast their happy eyes on this international film star, heralded by some fans as the most handsome and debonair actor in motion picture history.

"Thank you, thank you," Opie said, motioning for the crowd to sit after lengthy applause. "Hey, everybody! Answer me! You love Denver, don't you!" More cheers erupted, even louder than before, and I could tell that Opie was a true politician, a guy who knew how to say nothing particularly important-and get a thunderous reaction.

"Well, I don't usually do this type of thing," Opie said, his voice more like that of a 20-year-old than of his actual age, 43. "In fact, I've got to admit I've never introduced anyone at this type of function, and I've never spoken at such a gathering myself. But I flew all the way here, from South Africa-from the set of my newest movie, 'Warrior'-just to speak to you for a few moments today, to tell you about this man."

Hearing this, from beside me on dais Patty gripped my forearm tightly, and I knew this meant she was worried this movie star was about to rip me to shreds in public-for she had been well aware of my few run-ins with Opie.

"Ben Rivera is a man who stood his ground, when there were those of us-including myself-who did everything we could to have him fired from his job," Opie confessed. "Well, Ben stood up for what he believed in-and what he believed in was to fight for the right to research Ruth and Virgil, those lovers who lived so long ago. Ladies and gentlemen, I was a fool, and I was selfish, and I'm sorry for that. You see, I was afraid that Ben would find a truth, some detail about Virgil Ballard or even his brother Wesley Ballard, that would prevent me from making lots of money-from residuals on that award-winning film many of you saw, or might have heard about."

Once again, thunderous cheers erupted, so loud despite the relatively small size of the crowd of only a few hundred people that they sounded more like youngsters at a high school football rally than seasoned adults at what should have been a boring banquet.

"The truths that Ben has discovered these past few years made me worry, motivated by my own selfishness that digital-film sales on that picture would decrease-sharply decreasing my personal income," Opie said. "And you know that happened? For the first year, or so-although people might think otherwise-demand for that film actually did dry up. And during that period, I was bitter. That attitude changed in me, though, when I finally read Ben's latest book-chronicling the lives of Ruth and Virgil, a far more romantic story, I believe than even what once had been the legend of poet Wes Ballard and his girl. Why am I saying all this today, why am I admitting my own stupidity? Because, I need to be a man, like Ben Rivera has been for you. I need to say, to admit, and to shout out to the world that history matters-history matters, in our hearts and in our minds, because history makes us who we are, and who our ancestors will become. This is why, ladies and gentlemen, I would like to introduce you to the man I recommend you re-elect as your association president, Ben Rivera."

The crowd went wild with cheering. Some members even stood on their chairs, while holding placards: "Vote for Ben! 2 More Years!" They started hollering, "Ben! Ben! Ben! Ben!" and at that moment, I could think of nothing but Ruth and Virgil.

The moment their applause began to subside, I pushed a button at the podium. It turned on a gigantic roller machine on the ceiling. From the roller, a giant photograph of Ruth and Virgil emerged behind me, the image as huge as the wall-the size of a movie screen. It was a blowup of that same photo Annie had shown me three years ago.

"Ladies and gentlemen, your cheers should not be for me," I stressed. "I know we're all proud of these people, from so long ago, for the inspiration they've helped give to the world. And I realize what makes you delighted, what makes you proud, is that the publicity that stemmed from this research has given each of you, and even of your own departments from state-to-state, much-needed and much-deserved recognition.

"Before the public first heard of me, before they learned of my office's research into the Ballard case, just about nobody in the public knew what a state archivist is-did they? Before all this, you weren't appreciated, where you?" Catcalls of "yeah" and "you tell them, Ben" erupted.

"Well, I'll tell you what, my friends, what we all need to remember is our ancestors, those people like Ruth and Virgil. Like each of us do today, and like our children and grandchildren will in the future, each of these two lovers held a dream-the thought of achieving, of grasping onto a sense of happiness.

"And now that my office has proven inconclusively, beyond a shadow of a doubt that the 'Looking Back' poem actually was written by Virgil-I would like us all to take a few brief moments now to look back. Virgil was a hard-working, decent man, a loving man like each of us gentlemen should be today, the kind of person we should aspire to being. And to the end of her life, Ruth remained a loving, caring person cherished by her entire family, for she stood by all her relatives even when times got toughest, even when she found herself admitting to them all that she adored Virgil with all her heart.

I turned to the large blowup image, and pointed toward the couple-pictured in their teens, each youthful and vibrant, their expressions filled with love and hope, as if they sensed all great possibilities.

"No, they were not saints. No, they were not perfect. And, no, they could have done plenty of things better in life, just like each of us is not a saint, none of us are perfect, and almost all of us wish we could turn back time and eliminate our mistakes. But through it all, no matter where we go in life, we're like them-for we always have that hope for love. My dreams were realized, when I was reunited with my high school sweetheart, my wife, Patty."

The crowd cheered, for in the past few days, just about every one of them had met her, and she rapidly became a part of our collective archivist family-thanks, in part, to her cheerfulness.

"But these words I give today are not all peaches and cream, not all fun and roses. I have to tell you, that every question that anybody asks is 'stupid.'" At this point, I paused for effect, and noticed that many were giving quizzical expressions-as if trying to figure out what I meant. "Yes, everyone in the world might disagree with me, but all questions are 'stupid'-an assumption, on my part, that flies in the face of political correctness. Let me explain. It was a 'stupid question' for me to ask Wesley Bennett Fegley to attend today's banquet, but he came anyway." On queue, Wesley, his wife Doreen, and their grandchildren, Grace and Bennett, stood up in the audience-drawing loud cheers. With them, taking up an entire section of more than 35 tables, were many of the known descendants of those now famous lovers.

"Yes, the family, the offspring of Ruth and Virgil. Stand, please, Justin Ballard, U.S. Senator-elect from the state of Nevada," I began to rattle off most of the names, one by one, each generating just as much applause as the one before it. "Stand, please, Ruth Saunders Bixby, a key scientist in NASA's current Venus exploration program.

Stand, please, Bennett Thurston Ballard, a noted real estate agent from Reno, Nevada. Stand please, Annie Johns, now a motivational speaker based in Los Angeles."

As Annie stood she held the belt buckle far above her head, and the crowd became delirious with pleasure.

"Notice the belt buckle," I observed, as if I needed to say anything at all. "And stand, please . . ."

I went through just ten more, just enough of Ruth and Virgil's ancestors to drive the point home without having to read a virtual phonebook of names. I then, explained, briefly of how the erroneous legend began, misinformation concocted by author Marcus Melton-all to make the world believe that it had been Wesley, Virgil's brother, who wrote the poem.

"Let us remember, that each of us is a descendant of someone. Each of us is a product of the dreams, and aspirations of those who have lived so long ago. Like the Ballard descendants and like the Saunders descendants, each of us does his or her best to endure. When we-that is, when my team of researchers put on space suits-anti radio-active clothing to enter the Winnemucca zone last year-they risked their lives to find the truth. As many of us know, these brave researchers entered what had been known as the Sonoma Ranch, where Virgil had grown up and worked so hard. It was there, as we all know, that these tenacious researchers from my staff entered that home-and, in a hidden compartment under the floor of Virgil's old childhood room-they found the love letters, and the original poem, in his own handwriting, dated at the time his little brother, Wesley, was just halfway through elementary school.

"Yes, sometimes history wants to lie to us. Sometimes history wants us to ask 'stupid questions,' in hunting for the right answers. But like I say, all questions are 'stupid,' because we should never *have to ask* questions, we should only seek out answers. To me, this philosophy of mine is best understood by remembering that famous old line from the hit 1970s film that so many of us still enjoy watching today, 'Love Story.'

"It was Ryan O'Neill who uttered that still-famous line, 'Love means never having to say you're sorry.' Well, I argue that my morals, my values take all that just one step further, 'all questions are stupid.' Yes, all questions are stupid, when we as a society fight one another for living space, when we would be better off simply telling each other, 'I want to help you.' This is what I leave the association, for I would like to announce today-I need to announce-that even if you elect me, I must resign in just three months, because I'm retiring early from my job. I'm retiring because I have no more questions to ask of myself, or of the world. I'm retiring from my 'working job' because like Ruth and Virgil of so long ago-two people I shall always admire-I have a dream to make true. Life is too short to waste.... Thank you."

The ovations came in waves as I sat down. Back in my chair, I bowed my head, and I closed my eyes. As Patty clasped my hands, all I could think of were Ruth and Virgil, so long ago. I felt the sensations of them out on that hayride, telling each other of their undying love, of their commitment to spend their lives together. In thinking of them, I wasn't dwelling on the past, so much as I was dreaming of my own future. In our hearts, I believe, we are all young, virtually butterflies coming out of our cocoons no matter what stage in life. I took a long, deep breath, glad to be in good health. Then, those many handshakes began.

Virgil Ballard spent the first fifty years of his life as a Nevada cowboy spending many long hours in the saddle, breaking broncos, branding, fixing fences, and all such things that cowboys do. Later he established a successful real estate business with offices in Reno, Nevada, and other northern Nevada counties.

POETRY AVAILABLE
VOLUMES I & II OF POEMS
WRITTEN BY VIRGIL BALLARD
ARE AVAILABLE.
AN UNBELIEVABLE COLLECTION THAT WILL
TAKE YOU UP AND SOWN THE SCALE OF EMOTIONS.
MOST OF THEM WRITTEN WITH RUTH IN MIND.

FOR ORDERING INFORMATION CONTACT:
Trafford Pub.
OR virgil@ballard-company.com